Love You Forever

Love You Forever

(Eternal Love)

Julián Lorenzana

Copyright © Julián Lorenzana.

All rights reserved. No part of this book may be reproduced in any form or by any electronic or mechanical means, including information storage and retrieval systems, without permission in writing from the publisher, except by reviewers, who may quote brief passages in a review.

ISBN: 978-1-64921-198-9   (Paperback Edition)
ISBN: 978-1-64921-199-6   (Hardcover Edition)
ISBN: 978-1-64921-197-2   (E-book Edition)

Book Ordering Information

Phone Number: 347-901-4929 or 347-901-4920
Email: info@globalsummithouse.com
Global Summit House
www.globalsummithouse.com

Printed in the United States of America

Contents

Chapter 1 – Introduction 1
Chapter 2 – I Meet My Future Wife...3
Chapter 3 – Teresa and I Are Together Again.................................6
Chapter 4 – An Event to Forget...10
Chapter 5 – Teresa Becomes My Wife...14
Chapter 6 – Life As Newlyweds Begins...16
Chapter 7 – Six Weeks at Hi-Pass Camp..20
Chapter 8 – Our First Baby Lost...23
Chapter 9 – Birth and Death of Our Baby Boy.............................27
Chapter 10 – A Trio of Baby Girls..29
Chapter 11 – Teresa's Calvary Begins..34
Chapter 12 – Dyskinesia Sets In.. 44
Chapter 13 – Teresa in a Wheel Chair.. 46
Chapter 14 – Dementia Sets In 49
Chapter 15 – Dementia, Dyskinesia and Loss of Voice 57
Chapter 16 – Living with Leslie..59
Chapter 17 – Is It a Tumor or Not? 63
Chapter 18 – Frustration and Hopelessness 68
Chapter 19 – A Very Sad Farewell 72

Epilogue...75
About the Author 79

Chapter 1

Introduction

This is the story of two people who definitely were made for each other. I know because I am one of them. We were born in the same state of Jalisco, Mexico, approximately fifteen miles from each other. I came to the United States in 1945, at the age of twelve and a half, settling down in Brawley, California. She came to the United States in 1951, at the age of eleven, and also settled in Brawley. We both began our lives in the U. S. as illegal aliens. We both went through the grades, graduating from high school in 1955 and 1961 respectively.

While attending Imperial Valley Junior College in the 1955-1956 school year I received my draft notice and I soon entered the Army. At the same time, she was attending high school and selling dresses after school. She had become friends with my sister so, one day, she went to my house to try to sell a dress to my mother or to my sister. That was when she met me through a picture she saw displayed on the wall.

When I was released from the Army, in 1958, I was planning to get a permanent job because I didn't think I would be able to set my mind on my studies. But under my mother's urging and encouragement, I decided to resume my education and I soon got my AA degree. Junior college was as far as I had planned to go because I did not have the means to advance any further. The G. I. Bill had been abolished so I couldn't get help from the government. I had been offered a full-time job where I was working part-time after school. Fortunately, San Diego State University began offering some extension classes at my alma mater, Imperial Valley Junior College, so I decided to continue my education. Math had always been my forte but the only major offered was Education so I decided to become a teacher.

After completing my first year at San Diego State, I was offered a job teaching a combination class of sixth, seventh and eighth graders at Heber Elementary School and I took it, even though I still had a full year of college to complete.

Chapter 2

I Meet My Future Wife

During my first year of teaching, 1960-61, I decided to go to the show. There, I saw a very beautiful girl at the ticket booth and I decided to ask her out.

"Hi, there, miss. My name is Julián Lorenzana but you can call me Julio. I understand you are my sister's friend. Is that right?" I asked.

"Yes, I am," she answered. "My name is Teresa and you can call me Tere or Teresita. Why did you ask?" she inquired.

"Well, I'm her brother and I thought maybe you and I could become friends," I answered.

"Yes, I know who you are. I saw your picture when I went to your house to sell a dress to Luisa. She told me you were in the Army. Are you out already?" she wanted to know.

"Yes, I am. I've been out for some time," I told her. "Do you have a boyfriend?" I asked her.

"No, I don't have a boyfriend now," she answered. "Why do you want to know?" she asked.

"Well, I think you're the most beautiful girl in the world and I want to know if I can take you out," I stated. "How about it? Will you go out with me?" I asked.

"Sure, why not? When and where do you want to take me?" she eagerly asked.

"I like to watch movies, especially Mexican ones, so I thought I'd bring you here, where you work, this coming Saturday. Would you like that? Or we can go to either the Circle Theater or the Brawley Theater. I like American movies, too," I answered.

"Yes, we can come here on Saturday," she answered. "What time do you want to pick me up?" she asked.

"How does six o'clock sound?" I asked.

"Six o'clock sounds fine. I'll be ready," she assured me.

"Great! I'll see you Saturday," I told her excitedly.

Saturday came and I was very prompt at Teresa's house. Her mother, Mrs. Zendejas, greeted me at the door.

"Good afternoon, Julián. Teresa will be out in a while," she promised.

"Good afternoon, Mrs. Zendejas. I'll wait for her here," I said.

"Okay, that's fine," she assured me.

Very soon, Teresa came out, greeted me and told me, "We're ready!"

"We're ready? Who else is coming?" I inquired.

"It's only my sister, Nina. My mother wants her to come with us as sort of a chaperone. You don't mind, do you?" she asked.

"Of course not. It's okay. Let's go," I urged them. "Here, I'll open the door for you," I offered.

Once inside the theater, we selected a place to sit and, to my chagrin, Nina sat between Teresa and me, which was not to my liking. Before the movie started, I asked Nina, "Why are you sitting there? How am I going to talk to Teresa? Will you please sit where she is so that she can sit by me?" I begged.

"Sure, I can do that. I don't know why my mother told me to sit between you two," she said.

Once in our seats and the movie going, I put my arm around Teresa's shoulders and we tried to whisper to each other but it was impossible. I was sitting on her right and she had hearing problems with her right ear. I, on the other hand, had trouble hearing with my left ear.

When the movie was over, I took them home and I said good-bye to Teresa at the door of her house. I did not give her a kiss because I thought it was not appropriate on our first date. Besides, her mother was nearby watching us. I simply said good-bye and left.

Even though I liked Teresa a lot, a year passed before I saw her again. I had been too busy and too poor for our relationship to go anywhere, due to my concentration on my job, my classes three days a week and my financial situation.

Chapter 3

Teresa and I Are Together Again

During the middle of my second year of teaching, I began to think more seriously about Teresa and I decided to talk to her again, hoping she was free from any relationship. One day, after Sunday mass, I saw her walking home and I offered her a ride. She accepted and we spoke about many things. When we got to her house, before she got out of the car, I said to her, "I know I haven't asked you out in a long time but I don't want you to think that I don't like you. I like you a lot but, for various reasons, I thought it was better to leave you alone. But now, I can't see myself living without you in my life. How about us getting together again?"

"I'm sorry, Julián, but I can't do that. I have a boyfriend," she informed me.

"Oh, I'm sorry," I apologized. "Are you very much in love with him?" I inquired.

"Oh, no," she answered. "I like him and we get along very well. His name is Oscar and he lives in Calexico," she informed me.

"It sounds as if he is a nice guy," I said. "But would it break your heart if you broke up with him?" I audaciously asked.

"Why would I have to break up with him?" she asked. "I have no reason to do that," she added.

"Well, I would like for us to resume our relationship. I know I'm the one who neglected to call you after our first date. Believe me, it was tough on me. I've been thinking about you constantly since then. I just hadn't been ready to call you. I am now but I'm sorry you have a boyfriend and you can't break up with him," I confessed.

"I didn't say I couldn't break up with him!" she retorted. "I'm not really in love with him but why would I break up with him?" she asked.

"Well, so you can go out with me," I answered. "Will you go out with me?" I insisted.

"But how will I break up with Oscar?" she asked. "He is a very nice boy and I would feel bad if I broke his heart," she added.

"Well, I'm a nicer guy, even if I say so myself. Kidding aside, do you like me at least a little bit?" I asked.

"Well, yes, I think so," she answered sheepishly. "I think I've liked you since the day I went to your house to sell a dress to your sister. I also liked your singing in church," she confessed. "Oh, l like you alright but I always thought you did not like me, especially after you failed to call me again after our first date," she complained.

"You are wrong, Teresa. I still think you're the most beautiful girl in the world!" I assured her. "I already gave you my reason why I never called you again. It was cruel of me and a grave mistake. But now we know we like each other and we should renew our relationship, right?" I asked her.

"Yes, we will but I'll have to figure out a way to break up with Oscar gently. I'll have to see him in order to say good-bye to him. I think I would like to do it personally," she explained.

"But why do you have to see him?" I asked. "You can send him a Dear John letter. That will probably be easier on you. You won't feel bad if he cries about it," I suggested.

"I don't know how I will do it but I'll break up with him for sure," she assured me. "But are you sure you want us to get together again?" she asked.

"You'd better believe it! I'm quite serious. I would like it very much!" I assured her.

"Okay! You've convinced me. Call me in about five days," she insisted.

"I will. Now I'd better let you out before your mother comes and chases me away," I declared.

I let Teresa out and said, "Thank you for letting me drive you home. You've made my day! I'll call you Friday. Good-bye, Teresa."

"Good-bye, Julián. Thanks for the ride. Don't let me down again and call me, okay?" she begged.

"I won't let you down this time, believe me! I'll call you for sure," I assured her.

When Friday came, I called Teresa in the afternoon. When she answered, her voice made my heartbeat accelerate a little. I was really glad she was home.

"Hello. Is that you, Julián?" she asked.

"Yes, it's me. I told you I would call you. I won't mess up this time," I promised. "How are you? Do you have any good news for me?" I anxiously asked.

"I am fine, thank you," she answered. "How are you, Julio? What's up?" she asked.

"I'm fine, too, thank you," I answered. "I called to find out what happened with you and Oscar," I added.

"Well, everything is fine. Everything is over between him and me. I did send him a Dear John letter, as you suggested. Of course, he called me over the phone asking for explanations. Even though I gave him my reasons in the letter, he wanted to know if I really wanted to break up with him. He didn't like the idea but he said he would respect my decision and he wished us good luck," she explained.

"That's great! I'm sorry for him, of course, but I'm happy for me," I stated ecstatically. "Now, do you want to go to the show this Sunday? We'll go to any of the three shows you want," I promised.

"Yes, that will be great!" she answered. "We'll decide after mass, okay?" she added.

"Yeah," I answered. "See you after mass," I added.

"Okay, Julián. I'll see you then," she agreed.

The weeks and months went by rather quickly. Teresa and I took in many movies during that time, besides attending some of our friends' parties and going to a few formal dances, especially during the summer, when I had more free time to enjoy with her. And now we could go to our events without a chaperone. For some reason she had disappeared and we liked that much better.

Chapter 4

An Event to Forget

When the new school year began, our dates became more far apart because I was teaching full-time and I was attending college classes three days a week. I was also teaching English at night to non-English speakers two days a week. But whatever time we spent together, we enjoyed it tremendously. We had become so close that we began to talk about our future together. Most of our get-togethers were at her house, where we spent our time in her bedroom, with the door wide open. We turned on her record player and we danced away most of our time. She had never learned to dance because her mother never allowed her to visit her girlfriends or to go to dances. I've always been considered a pretty good dancer so I became her dance teacher.

Sometime during the school year 1961-62, Teresa and I decided we couldn't stay away from each other. We decided to get married on May 12 so we announced it to our parents. My mother and my sister were elated but her mother didn't seem to be happy.

After the wedding date was announced, things began to change between Teresa's mother and me, even between them. This did not surprise us. Her mother had often abused Teresa physically and emotionally while she was a little girl and even into adolescence and adulthood. Her neighbors would try to come to her rescue but her mother always told them it was none of their business.

On a certain day, apparently after having been abused, Teresa's sister, Nina, gave me a call.

"Julián, my mother wants you to come for Teresa! She says she doesn't want her in our house anymore! Hurry and come pick her up!" she said.

"Are you serious, Nina? She wants me to go pick up Teresa and bring her to my house?" I asked.

"Yes, she is very serious. She is angry over something." she answered.

"Okay. I'll be there in twenty minutes!" I promised.

I went to pick her up and found her in tears. I asked her, "What happened and why does your mother want me to take you to my house?"

"My little brother fell and she blamed me for it. She said I should have been keeping an eye on him. She expects me to be everywhere. I was ironing in my room and he fell in the living room. I tried to tell her that I was ironing in my room but she would not even let me talk. Instead, she hit me with the broom. I'm glad she wants to get rid of me. I'd rather be with you than here in my house," she said.

"I would like nothing better than to take you to my house but that would not look proper. I will take you to my sister's house instead, okay? You'll be okay there until we get married. You will see me every day. I'm sorry about your relationship with your mother. But remember, I will be able to see you every day without asking for her permission," I said.

"Okay, Julián. Whatever you say is okay with me," she said.

One day, on my mother's birthday, Luisa was making a cake for my mother and she found out that some ingredient was missing. She had to go to her house to get it so I drove her, my mother and my brother-in-law to her house, leaving only my niece, Hilda, with Teresa. When we returned, my niece ran out of the house to tell me that Mrs.

Zendejas was mistreating Teresa. When I got inside the house, I found that she had Teresa by the hair, on the floor. I confronted her and took Teresa away from her. As I did, she kicked me on the shin bone, with no consequence. But I did yell at her, "What the devil were you doing? "Why were you mistreating her? Haven't you gotten tired of mistreating her?" I asked her in a strong voice.

"It's none of your business! I came to take her because I felt like it! She doesn't belong here because you two aren't married yet!" she shouted.

"No, we haven't gotten married but you asked me to pick her up because you did not want her in your house anymore! Don't you remember? Well, if Teresa does not want to go with you, you cannot force her to go!" I informed her.

"Well, I'm going to take her even if she doesn't want to go!" she argued.

"Well, I'm sorry, ma'am, but you can't! And now, leave my house, please! If you don't leave, I'll have to call the police!" I threatened her.

I did have to call the police because she was still belligerent and refused to vacate my house. Two of them came right away and the first thing one of them asked Teresa was, "How old are you, young lady?"

"I'm twenty-one. I don't know why she kicked me out of her house a few weeks after we announced that Julian and I would soon get married," she informed them.

"Why did she come to this house?" one of the officers asked.

"A few weeks ago, Teresa's sister, Nina, called me to tell me that her mother did not want her sister in the house anymore. She said that her mother wanted me to go pick her up and bring her to my house. Knowing her habit of abusing Teresa and two of her siblings, I assumed she had been abused so I went to pick her up right away. But now she is trying to force her to return home and my fiancée doesn't want to go back. I had taken my mother and my sister to her house for some ingredient she needed to make a cake and when we returned, I found Teresa on the floor with her mother's hands on her hair, apparently being abusive right here in my house. I separated them and, as I did, Mrs. Zendejas kicked me." I explained.

Right away, the other policeman asked Mrs. Zendejas, "Do you speak English, ma'am?"

"Yes, I do," answered Mrs. Zendejas.

"Ma'am, your daughter is over 21 and you cannot force her to go with you. I think you should go back to your house. After what happened here, we may have to take you with us if your daughter lodges a complaint against you for abusing her and Mr. Lorenzana can lodge another one for kicking him." the policeman told her.

Mrs. Zendejas and Nina left the premises, but not before Mrs. Zendejas hurled a few expletives in my direction, which I ignored.

Chapter 5

Teresa Becomes My Wife

After my confrontation with Mrs. Zendejas, everything went smoothly. We decided to get married on March 3, two months before the original date. We spoke with Father Valbuena and he approved the date. Preparations began in earnest. The meetings with the priest, the selection of our sponsors and of our grooms and bridesmaids, the food menu, the musicians and the list of guests were taken care of. All the activities, except for the wedding itself, were to take place at Hidalgo Hall.

At times, the preparations became rather hectic and stressful. I couldn't be at all the places that required my presence because I was busy with my college classes and my homework, on top of my teaching activities. I had to delegate some chores and all the personnel involved were very good about it.

The day arrived and the whole thing became even more hectic as some people were late to their assignments. Some of those assignments were switched as some people had forgotten who was to pick up what or whom. But, eventually, everything was ready, except for the bride.

Whoever was to pick her up was a little late at the church. I could have picked her up myself but I wasn't allowed to do so because of the bad luck taboo that the groom should not see the bride in her wedding dress until she walks to the altar and is given to him.

When the bride finally arrived, the people clapped, the pianist began the processional and she, at her brother Emilio's elbow, and her bridesmaids and the bridegrooms began to walk toward the front. The church choir provided the singing during the ceremony. As the ceremony ended, the priest spoke a few words of encouragement, the recessional began and my wife and I, along with the rest of the members of the wedding, walked out with a thunderous applause accompanying our steps. The church was emptied as we all rushed to Hidalgo Hall, where the festivities continued.

When everybody was in the hall, a few announcements were made and the master of ceremonies, who happened to be the leader of the band, called for Teresa and me to be ready to begin our special dance piece. The music began the song "Está Sellado" and we began to dance. After a few steps, I ceded Teresa to her brother and my mother came to me and we continued the dance. There continued an exchange of dancing partners, as the song continued. A little after Teresa and I came back together, the song ended and we all sat down.

After our special song, the band went into a series of dance numbers, enjoyed greatly by all. Teresa and I happily danced almost every piece, sometimes simply holding on tightly and swinging sideways as we were mighty tired. Just before the dance ended, the padrinos (sponsors) cut the cake and almost everybody enjoyed a little piece. The music continued for another hour. When the music ended, we thanked the musicians and they bid Teresa and me good-bye and a happy life together. We left my mother, the padrinos and a few of the brides and grooms to clean up after us, as planned beforehand. Nobody wished us a happy honeymoon trip because we had let everybody know that we would simply go home to sleep. I had to do my preparation for the next week of school. We told them that our honeymoon trip would take place during our summer vacation, if that was what we wished.

Chapter 6

Life As Newlyweds Begins

Life as newlyweds was great but instances of disharmony showed their ugly face often, especially during the first few years. Nights were almost always blissful and magical but when mornings came, we were forced to face the realities of life, some of which were discouraging.

"Good morning, my beautiful wife. How is the most beautiful wife in the world?" I greeted.

"Good morning, sweetheart. I feel great!" she answered. "Please cut out the flattery. There are millions, maybe billions, of very beautiful wives in the world so I cannot be the most beautiful. Save your flattery for tonight. They won't get you anywhere right now," she commanded.

"But to me you're the most beautiful of all of those billions of wives. Do you know that I love you more than anything in the world? Of course, you do. I've been telling you that for years. Or is it months? I've lost count. Anyway, you are my Maria Felix," I declared.

"I love you, too, Julián, and you are my Pedro Infante," she added. (María Felix, a very beautiful lady and Pedro Infante, a very handsome singer, were Mexico's leading movie stars.)

"What are we going to do today? I'm ready for anything you want to do!. Let's get up and then we will decide," she added.

"Wait a minute! Didn't you just say you are ready for anything I want? Let's not get up! Let's cuddle up some more," I demanded.

"Julián! What are you insinuating? Haven't you had enough? Let's get up to eat breakfast. It's already eight o'clock in the morning. We have a life ahead of us. Come on, honey!" she begged.

"Okay, sweetheart, I guess I can wait. Let's get up," I agreed.

A month after our marriage, we were invited to a friendly get-together at one of our closest friend's house. Ray and Lupe Rodríguez had gotten married a few years before us and they invited us to their house. When we got to their house, there were three other couples waiting for us. We greeted them and we made ourselves at home. A record player was turned on and, as the music began, we all got up to dance. The host couple suggested we exchange dance partners. The night was very pleasant. We danced all night and I danced with all the ladies present. What I did wrong was dance with the other ladies more than I danced with Teresa and she let me have it when we got home.

"Why did you dance with the other girls more than you did with me?" she exploded as we got inside the house. "I thought you loved me so much!" she complained.

"I'm really sorry, honey! I didn't realize I had done that. Forgive me. You are right. I did neglect you. I was enjoying myself so much I didn't realize I was doing it. Some of the songs were fast-paced and you don't like to dance those. You like to dance only the slow ones and the fast ones are my favorites. I'm sorry. The next time we go out to dance, I will remember to sit those out," I promised.

"No, no, no, no! Please don't pay any attention to me! I get a little jealous seeing you spinning those girls around when you dance those corridos. I'm sorry I'm not a good dancer. I wish I could dance those fast ones so that you could spin me around instead of somebody else," she confessed.

"It's okay, Tere. I should be more sensitive to your feelings. But I assure you, there's nothing wrong about me dancing with somebody else. You know you're my María Felix and I love you. Please remember that, okay? With me teaching you, you'll be an expert at those fast ones. Then, I will spin no one else but you," I promised.

"I know. Let's forget about the whole thing, okay?" she said.

"Okay. It's forgotten. Let's get ready to go to sleep. It's very late," I suggested.

March and April went by quite rapidly, I thought, and, despite a few bad times when we argued over silly, unimportant things, life was great to us. My days at work were as pleasant as always, except for the fact that I was always anxious to get home to see my beautiful wife.

Today is May 7 and Tere's birthday is on Sunday, May 9, so tomorrow we begin to make plans to celebrate it.

"What do you want to do tomorrow? Do you want to go out for dinner?" I asked Tere. "We can go to a restaurant," I suggested.

"No, no. Let's stay home and prepare something here. I already have the cake in the refrigerator. It's still early. We have plenty of time to go to the store to get the ingredients necessary," she said.

"You already made the cake? Why didn't you tell me so I could get a piece?" I complained.

"Because I was afraid you would do just that. It's a good thing you didn't see it in the freezer or you would have gotten a taste," she said.

"Are you sure you wouldn't rather go to a restaurant? I wouldn't want you to work too hard. You already prepare my breakfast every morning and you also prepare my lunch every day. I love it but it's too much work for you. You should allow me to take you out so you can rest," I told her.

"No, Julio. Don't worry about me working too hard every morning, day or night. I love keeping our house clean and I love cooking for you. Let's stay home. I won't mind preparing a mole poblano and rice dish for us. I want to do it because I know that is your favorite dish. Okay?"

she asked. "We'll invite only your mother's and your sister's families," she added.

"Okay. You've got me sold on the mole poblano. I can already taste the mole in my mouth. Let's go to the store now," I suggested.

"Okay, let's go," she agreed.

The next morning, a Saturday, we both got up early and, after breakfast, she quickly began her work on the mole poblano. I helped her in whatever I could. At times, I would sit and watch TV while she hummed a tune as she worked. At other times, I would get up, grab her in my arms, from behind so as not to interfere with her hands, and give her a few kisses. It was blissful and she enjoyed every minute of it! She was working hard and I was enjoying her body with my hands. I knew I shouldn't have been interrupting her work but I couldn't help it. She was so tempting and she didn't mind the interruptions. She would simply giggle and slap my hands whenever I got a little too daring. By one o'clock, everything was ready and so was my stomach. A little later the guests arrived.

"Sweetheart, how anxious are you to hit your mole poblano?" she asked.

"I'm very anxious and very hungry, honey! Can I sit at the table now?" I asked.

"Yes, you can. I'll serve us in a minute," she answered.

We all sat at the table and enjoyed our delicious mole poblano, a popular Mexican dish. After eating, we sang happy birthday to Tere and ate the cake. Everything turned out very well. Mom and my sister wanted to go home after we ate but I asked them to stay a little longer because I had some news to share with everybody.

Tere whispered in my ear, "Sweetheart, I'm ready to go to bed. I'm tired but I feel like cuddling with you for a while before going to sleep."

"Wait, sweetheart. I'm as anxious to cuddle as you are but we'll go to bed in a little while. I want to tell everyone here what we plan to do during this summer," I told her.

"Hey, that sounds intriguing and mysterious. What are we going to do during the summer?" she asked.

Chapter 7

Six Weeks at Hi-Pass Camp

"You know who my principal is, don't you?" I asked.

"Yes, I do," she answered.

"Well, he was asked to conduct a summer camp for children up in the mountains, near Campo, in July. It will be called Hi-Pass Camp and it will last six weeks. He will be the Director and I will be his Assistant Director. I agreed to do it but you have the last word, Tere, because you will be coming along. If you are not up to it, I'll tell him I can't help him. What do you think?" I asked her. "The kids will have several activities a day that includes a long hike during the second week," I added.

"It sounds great! We will get lots of sun and exercise," she said excitedly.

"Wouldn't that be too hard on Teresa?" asked Mother.

"She'll be okay," sis interrupted. "She's young and walking is supposed to be good, even for a pregnant woman. As long as she doesn't overdo it," she added. "But she's not pregnant yet, is she?" she asked.

"Not yet. I've missed a period but I don't think I am," she answered.

"Okay. I guess it will be alright," Mother agreed. "Good luck on that endeavor!" she added.

Monday came and Tere went to see the doctor, who confirmed her pregnancy and when I came back from work, she quickly gave me the good news.

"Julio, I found out today that I am, indeed, pregnant. The doctor confirmed it. Isn't it great?" she asked.

"Yes, it is, sweetheart," I answered elatedly. "I love you, honey! Will you be okay working at Hi-Pass Camp?" I asked.

"I'll be okay. I will take care of myself," she assured me.

The day came and we drove up to Campo full of anticipation. When we got to camp, Mr. Frantz and his wife, the nurse, were already there and they welcomed us.

"We're going to enjoy this outing, Julián," said Mr. Frantz.

"I agree," echoed Mrs. Frantz.

"I hope so," I said. "I hope we can escape a bad case of heatstroke. Don't forget that July is one of the hottest months of the summer. But if we take the proper precautions, I'm sure we will be okay. Besides, we're up in the mountains," I injected.

"Don't worry, honey. "We'll be okay," Tere said.

"Hey, honey, I was afraid you wouldn't want me to do it. But I'm glad you agreed. We're not only getting sun and exercise. We're both getting paid. You will be working with the kids, too," I informed her.

The first two weeks of summer camp went by without any problems. Our relationship with the kids was great but I can't say the same thing about the children's relationship with the nurse, Mrs. Frantz. She was so overbearing that many of the kids were at odds with her. That made the relationship between her and Mr. Frantz worse than it had normally been. It was generally known that there were problems between them and their stay at the camp was making things worse. Even Tere was having problems with her.

The day of the hike came and we made the proper preparations for it. We gathered at the front of the cabins. We assigned groups of children to their respective supervisors. We discussed the proper precautions to prevent injuries, including possible encounters with venomous snakes.

We began the trek and, while on it, we encountered several wild animals, including coyotes, squirrels, and rattlesnakes. We explored some caves and played some music on the way, to which some children enjoyed dancing.

The trek ended with a splash in the swimming pool and later on, the children broke a piñata. It was really successful and quite enjoyable, despite the tired feeling a lot of the children and some of the adults felt.

Chapter 8

Our First Baby Lost

As enjoyable as our Hi-Pass experience was, the trek did have bad side effects on Tere and me. Before we went to bed the night of the trek, Tere said to me, "Honey, I don't feel good! I need to go to the bathroom!" She went in and I waited for her outside. Suddenly, she screamed, "Julián, come inside, please!"

"What's the matter?" I asked.

"Look, I'm bleeding! I thought I was only peeing but I felt something come out that made a splash on the toilet! As I flushed it, I saw something that made me think that it was my baby. Isn't it terrible! I think we've lost our baby!" she cried.

"Please don't worry, honey. Let's get ready to go to the hospital. Right now, I'll put you in bed so you can rest for a while," I told her.

Tere lay in bed and she soon fell asleep. That gave me a chance to go see Mr. Frantz to have a talk with him. When he saw me, he asked, "Are there any problems, Julián?"

"Mr. Frantz, I'm afraid I will have to leave you alone for a while. Teresa has some problems and we think she lost our baby. Because she lost a lot of blood and because of her state of mind, I'll have to take her to the hospital. I hope you don't mind," I explained.

After I explained what had happened, he agreed and said, "Julián, I think you should take her to the emergency room at the hospital. She may be okay but you'd better take her to make sure."

"If she's okay, I'll be back some time tomorrow. I'll call you after she sees the doctor and he tells me that she's okay," I promised.

When I returned to the cabin, Tere was awake and crying. I got her inside the car and she continued to cry for a few minutes. I looked at her for a second and gave her a kiss on her cheek. Then we sped to the hospital.

As soon as we got to the hospital, I took her to the emergency section, where she was quickly taken in. A doctor saw her and asked her, "What happened to you, young lady? I understand you lost your baby. Did you feel too tired at the end of the hike? Your husband told me about the hike," he told her.

"Yes, I did but I did not feel bad," she answered. "I was told that walking was good for a pregnant woman," she added.

"Well, it is if it's not too strenuous. But a five-mile hike may have been a little too much for you. But I don't think the hike caused your problem. Perhaps something else was the culprit. We'll never know. The good thing is that you are okay and ready for another pregnancy. Just make sure you take good care of yourself next time, okay?" he told her.

"Okay, doctor, I will. Can we go home now?" she asked.

"I'll have them prepare the necessary papers for you to go home. You'll be going home in a few minutes," he promised.

"Okay, doctor. Thank you," she said.

Forty minutes later, we were home and Tere went to bed right away and fell asleep. I looked at her, gave her a kiss and thanked God she was okay.

The next morning, Tere and I had a long conversation.

"Honey, I think you should not go back to the camp. I'm going to leave you with my mother. It's only four more weeks anyway. I'll be back home real soon. You'll be okay with my mother. What do you say?" I asked.

"I don't know. I want to be with you. I'm okay, sweetheart. I don't know for how long your mother can stand my presence and vice versa," she answered.

"You lost a lot of blood!" I told her. "I would rather you stay and recuperate here, instead of at the camp," I said.

"Okay. I'll stay for a few days but I will join you at the camp soon," she said.

Tere stayed at my mother's house for one week but she soon called me to tell me she was going to take the bus and join me at the camp because she missed me. I missed her too so I told her it was okay if that was what she wanted. I gave her some directions as to where she should get off the bus.

A few minutes before the bus was to arrive at the designated place, west of Campo, I went to wait for her. I knew what time the bus was to arrive but when it arrived, she did not get off. I became quite worried because there was no other bus scheduled to stop there so I drove toward Campo hoping I would find her there. As I got to Campo, I saw a lady with a suitcase walking westward. I heard some dogs barking close by and I thought that the lady would be bitten. I drove toward her and, as soon as she recognized the car, she yelled, "Julián! Julián! Julián! It's me!" I stopped the car and quickly got her in.

"What were you doing walking aimlessly in the middle of the street with those dogs barking? Why did you get off the bus here at Campo instead of at the designated place?" I asked her angrily.

"I didn't know where to get off. I thought the bus wouldn't stop again until it got to San Diego. I'm sorry, Julián," she apologized.

"Okay, okay. I'm sorry I yelled at you. I was afraid some dog would bite you. Let's go to the camp," I told her.

Our stay at the children's summer camp ended without any more bad consequences. It was a triumphant end to a period of great entertainment, laced with a few hardships.

Late in 1962, she miscarried again. That time I cried with her because I thought we weren't meant to be parents but, fortunately, I was wrong.

Soon, something happened that changed our lives. Four of my aunt Chita's children were taken away from her because of her heavy drinking. The two oldest were placed with my mother and the youngest ones, Angela and Raymond, were placed with us. We soon got very close to them as we got along beautifully. During this time, Teresa surprised me with some good news.

"Julio, guess what! I think I'm pregnant again! I haven't seen the doctor but I'm almost sure I am," she said.

"Are you sure, honey? Let's not count our blessings until you see the doctor and he tells you that you are, for sure, okay?" I told her.

"Okay. I won't say anything anymore until I see him," she agreed.

Four days later, Tere was told by her gynecologist that she was, indeed, pregnant and we were quite happy. We tried desperately to shoo away the ever-present fear of losing a baby that was always with us.

Chapter 9

Birth and Death of Our Baby Boy

About six months later, Teresa felt water spilling down one of her legs and she thought she was peeing but she soon realized that the baby was coming three months ahead of schedule. I rushed her to the hospital, where the doctor had to perform a Cesarean section to get the baby out. We were elated, especially because it was a boy. But that elation didn't last very long because on the third day, the day Teresa was to be released from the hospital, we were informed that our baby had died of some disease that hits preemies. I found Teresa inconsolable and we cried together for a little while.

After our little cry, I reminded her that God must have taken our baby for some reason only known to Him. I also reminded her that we were young and that we still had lots of time to have more babies. I held her close to me until she was able to get out of her sadness. The fact that it was the day she and the baby were scheduled to go home made her feel worse.

The months went by with us following practically the same routine. I continued working at my regular job, plus taking classes at San Diego

State University three days a week. I also taught English to non-English speaking adults the other two nights, in El Centro, fifteen miles away from Brawley. It was an arduous week but Tere and I were happy.

One day, after two more miscarriages in 1964, Teresa came to me and said, "You know, honey, I don't think I'll ever carry a baby the required nine months so maybe I shouldn't try to get pregnant."

"Don't say that, sweetheart. I'm sure one of these times God will allow you to do exactly that, carry a baby the nine months. You'll see. Don't give up the idea. We'll keep on trying. You do want a family, don't you?" I asked her.

"Of course, I do," she answered. "But I'm getting tired of losing the babies all the time!" she explained. "If it weren't for Raymond and Angela, my life would be less meaningful. I'm sure glad they're here," she added.

Chapter 10

A Trio of Baby Girls

While Raymond and Ángela were with us, Teresa became pregnant again and we were ecstatic. We prayed that this time everything would be okay.

Nine months later, on September 21, 1965, our baby, Lilián Teresa, was born and every one in our extended family was very happy. Unfortunately, a few months later our foster children were returned to my aunt. We had gotten along beautifully with them so it hurt to lose them but I am sure that their leaving would have been a greater loss if our child had not been born and doing well.

With the departure of my nephew and my niece, we were able to concentrate our attention on our baby girl. She grew into a beautiful and healthy little girl and we were as proud of her as we could be. Tere was happier than she had been for the last three years. And I couldn't be happier with my two girls.

Three years later, on April 2, 1968, our second daughter, Susan Lucille, was born. I was somewhat disappointed because I wanted a boy but that disappointment soon left with the pleasure of playing with my two little girls.

One day, I came home from work and found Tere on the floor playing with our two little girls. She turned to me and said, "Isn't it great that we already have our two daughters, honey? Now all we need is our two little boys to complete the foursome we had planned when we first got married."

"Yes, sweetheart, I agree," I answered. "Let's just hope and pray that God allows us to complete that foursome," I added.

Two years later, on October 11, our third child, Leslie Celine, was born. As soon as we brought her home, Tere asked me, "Are you terribly disappointed, sweetheart? Look at her! She has come to mess up our idea of two and two but isn't she beautiful?"

"Yes, she is and I am a little disappointed! But I don't care about the two and two idea anymore! As long as the babies and you are well, I'm happy," I answered.

I knew we would not be able to complete a foursome of two boys and two girls because we already had three girls but I thought we were young and we still had a chance of having at least one boy.

We were young, alright, but the next time Teresa went to see her gynecologist, he gave her some really bad news. Because all our four babies had been born by Cesarean Section, she was told that it would be dangerous to have more children. When she told me the news, she began to cry. You can guess how I felt. I had always hoped we would have a baby boy someday.

As the years went by, Teresa thought I was miserable because I didn't have a son. She would often ask me, "Julio, how about us adopting a little boy? There are so many children up for adoption and you are already a terrific father. How about it? Think about it."

"I've thought about it, honey, but I've decided not to because, if we adopt and he turns into a juvenile delinquent, I will regret it. I will blame it on his genes instead of on how we raised him. Besides, I'm quite happy with my three beautiful girls. I may eventually regret not adopting, especially if I don't have anybody to help me clean the yard or do other chores when I become old and dilapidated. But I'll bear every burden I won't get help with. Let's forget the whole thing and don't feel sorry for me. I'll be okay," I explained.

Our girls were growing up and, as they began to go to school, they began to experience the disappointments and achievements that beset children in general. But the achievements they earned made our lives more pleasant.

Life went on, with its ups and downs always making our existence either happier or sadder. There were countless ups that made our lives more enjoyable, especially the instances that afforded us, as parents, pride and satisfaction about what our girls accomplished or wished to accomplish.

Teresa and I had been members of our church choir for some time and, consequently, our three girls always accompanied us to church and learned to sing some of our songs. They also enjoyed watching the organist play the organ and listening to what came out of the organ. So, one day, I asked them, "How would you girls like to, one day, sing in the choir or play the organ?"

"Hey, that would be neat!" Lilián, the oldest one, answered. "I think I would like that very much!" she added.

"Not me!" exclaimed Susan, the middle one. "I like to hear the organ playing but I would rather just sing. It would be easier than learning to play it," she added.

"I don't know what I want to do," Leslie, the youngest one, stated. "I'm too young to decide but I do like the singing," she added.

"Well, I'll tell you what. We'll buy a piano, not an organ, so that all three of you can learn to play it. Later, you will decide what you want to do," I declared.

"That's a great idea. You may not decide to continue with piano lessons but it would be nice to have a piano at home. Even Dad may decide to learn to play it. He knows a little about note reading, right, honey?" Tere piped in.

"Yes, I will take lessons, but only if I have enough time and money. I am more interested in having the children learn to play it," I answered.

The three girls and I took lessons from my ex-high school choir teacher but they lasted only two years. The girls claimed that the teacher hit them on their hands whenever they made a mistake. For that reason, the two youngest ones begged me to let them discontinue the lessons, so I did. Not many children will be successful in whatever they are forced to do. As for me, I quit, too, when the teacher expected me to play an easy version of Ave Maria, a piece she usually accompanied me on the organ when I was asked to sing it at weddings. I didn't think I would learn it and, since the girls had quit, I followed suit. Lilián continued taking lessons for a while but she soon quit, too. She continued practicing what she had learned and, eventually, she was able to accompany our choir on the organ, following easy versions of the hymns I would prepare for her, using mainly two-finger accompaniment. She did it until she got married and moved to another city.

We did not raise any accomplished pianists but we all enjoy playing our own versions of our favorite songs on the ever-present piano. Even after their marriages, both Lilian and Leslie bought a piano and each of them played their piano for their own and their families' pleasure. In my case, our piano served as my partner in the writing of over seven hundred songs. Eventually, I had to sell our house and the piano because Tere and I had to move into Leslie's house.

In retrospect, Tere and I are mighty proud of the accomplishments of all the members of our family. Tere and the three girls graduated from our local Imperial Valley Community College. The three girls then graduated from San Diego State University with a Bachelor's Degree and a teaching credential. Teresa was diagnosed with Parkinson's disease and couldn't continue her education. I, too, got my AA degree at our local college and was able to continue on to San Diego State University, where I earned my Bachelor's Degree in Liberal Studies, my teacher's credential and my Master's Degree in Bilingual Education. Leslie was able to get her Master's Degree in the Arts later on.

God gave me the ability to sing and, though I didn't strive to get into the entertainment world, I did write over seven hundred songs, eighteen of which I recorded semi-professionally and others have been sung in church services.

Sometime in the 70's, I took a correspondence course in children's literature and I have written six stories. Three are for young children and the other three are for adolescents and for adults. They all have been published. The ending of the sixth one was up in the air for a while. I was at a point where I did not know how it would end. It is based on our married life and, since we are getting up there in age and we both have medical problems, I was going to leave it up to my daughter to finish it as soon as we both are gone. But I had it published even though we were both still alive. Now that Teresa has passed away, I will have it republished with a different ending.

At the beginning, we didn't think we were going to be allowed to become parents but God was good to us and He allowed us to raise three terrific daughters. We grew old with them and, in the process, we became proud of their achievements. We saw them graduate from grammar school, from our local junior college and from San Diego State University. All three earned their Bachelor's Degrees and their teaching credentials. Leslie even went further and earned her Master's Degree in the Arts.

Later on, we had the pleasure of witnessing their marriages and the births of all our eight grandchildren. The sad part is that I probably won't be around to see the last two of them graduate, even from grammar school.

We realize we have had a full life, full of happiness, albeit with great medical hardships, especially Tere. We pray to God that as soon as one of us goes to see Him, the other one will follow very soon after. Hopefully, once with God, our love will continue without any sad events.

Chapter 11

Teresa's Calvary Begins

Throughout our married life, we have enjoyed many happy events. The happiest events I have mentioned already and all of them gave us great satisfaction and enjoyment, even though most of them happened while we were under a cloud that came to somewhat obscure that enjoyment. That cloud appeared one day, in 1982, while we were at the table eating. I noticed that Tere's hand was shaking slightly, which was unusual.

"What's wrong with your hand, Tere?" I asked her.

"I don't know why but it started shaking yesterday," she answered.

"Why didn't you tell me? I hadn't noticed it shaking until today. I don't think it's normal. We'd better see Dr. Suárez about it. I'll take a day off from work tomorrow so we can see him, okay?" I told her.

"Okay, honey. I hope it's nothing serious," she said.

After a few tests were performed, the doctor told us it was something called Parkinson's disease and he explained the symptoms and some of the things Teresa would have to go through. He also set up an appointment with a neurologist in San Diego.

When we got home, Tere was inconsolable.

"Did you hear what is going to happen to me as I grow older? It's awful! Why did it have to happen to me? Why did God give me this awful disease? What did I do to deserve it?" she complained between sobs.

"I don't know, sweetheart. But don't cry. Right now, you're okay. It's only a little shaking. Let's hope it doesn't get much worse," I answered.

"But the doctor said it would get worse, didn't he?" she asked.

"Yes, he did. But he is not a neurologist. He doesn't know very much about the disease. Let's wait for the appointment with the neurologist. He will explain to us how the disease works," I told her.

Our appointment date to San Diego came and the neurologist gave us a worse picture of the ravages of the disease and Teresa became even more worried. He said that the shaking usually gets worse and that the muscles of the body get so bad she would eventually lose her mobility. As for the shaking, he said a new procedure was being worked on where, if taken, the shaking would disappear. With all that ominous information, we went back home.

Teresa was not herself for a few days as she kept thinking about the ravages of the disease. But she soon forgot about them and became her usual active and joyful self as she hoped the progression of the disease would be slow.

Tere's fear for what was to come in the future began to disappear but something else occurred in 2001 that came to plant fear in the minds of everyone in the family again. This time it was my turn to spend days and nights worrying. I had been having trouble empting my bladder for a while so I decided to tell Teresa about it.

"Tere, I didn't want to tell you but I have been having trouble emptying my bladder and I have to go see Dr. Suárez to see if something can be done," I told her.

"Of course, honey. You'd better have a check-up as soon as possible. Let's hope that some medicine can help you," she stated.

I went to see Dr. Suárez the next day and he prescribed Flomax as he told me, "This will make it easier for you to empty your bladder but it won't cure the problem. You'll be okay for a while but if you notice it getting worse, you'd better come and see me so I can check you again," he warned me. "Let's hope for the best!" he added.

For about two years I had no bad problems. I simply took the Flomax and I felt okay. But that was not to last. Soon, I had to go to the doctor's office to have my prostate checked again. The news he gave me was not encouraging. It was worrisome, to say the least. "Julián, I'm sorry to tell you that I felt a lump in your prostate and, to be on the safe side, I will refer you to a specialist in San Diego. He will tell you if that lump is benign or cancerous. I will set up an appointment with him as soon as possible. We'll call you to let you know when you should go see him."

"Okay, doctor, I'll expect to hear from you soon. Thank you," I said.

The next day, the doctor's office called me to give me the date of the appointment and a week later, Teresa and I went to San Diego to see the specialist, Dr. Lewis, who called me into his office as soon as we got there. Two tests were done and, soon after, he sent us home after he told us he would call me himself to tell me the results of the tests.

A week later, I received the specialist's phone call and I anxiously awaited his verdict. "Julián," he said. "I'm afraid I have bad news. The tests show that you do have cancer in your prostate and we have to decide what we're going to do. There are a few options you can choose from to take care of your problem. Before you come back to see me to tell me what choice you will take, I suggest you buy a certain book that will give you lots of information about cancer in the prostate. It will help you make your choice."

After a long silence on my part, I told him, "Okay, doctor, we'll see you soon. Thank you."

The bad news got me quite panicky. I have always been a hypochondriac so I thought the worst would happen to me, besides the terrible side effects of chemotherapy. Seeing the worry on my face, Teresa asked, "What is the matter? Why the worried look on your face? Did the doctor give you bad news?"

"Yes, sweetheart, I'm afraid so! Dr. Lewis said that I have cancer in the prostate and that I must go see him as soon as possible so we can talk about the options I have. He thinks the cancer has not metastasized and that we have a good chance of eliminating it, depending on the option I choose.

"What are those options?" she asked.

"In the book he told me to buy, which I did, I read about four options and the best one, if the cells have not spread to other parts of the body, is to take out the prostate completely. We will discuss those options when we see him. He wants me to go see him next week," I informed her.

"Today is Thursday so when next week?" she inquired.

"He told me to be there on Tuesday at 10 a.m. so we'll be there," I answered.

Tuesday came and we all went to San Diego. Very soon after we got to his office, he took us in and the discussion began.

"Okay, Julián, have you read the book I told you to buy?" he asked me.

"Yes, I did and I read it," I answered.

"Well, you are aware of the options you have, right?" he asked.

"Yes, I am but can you explain each one a little bit more, please. Two of them are quite simple but the others are more complicated," I said.

After his explanation of each option, he asked me, "Have you decided on one of them?"

"Well, since you have told me that you don't think the cancer has spread, we have chosen the radical prostatectomy, hoping that all the cancerous cells are still within the prostate," I explained.

"Have you thought about the possible side effects?" he asked.

"Yes, I have. All the options have terrible side effects but getting rid of the cancer is my main concern so I will take the prostatectomy over the others," I told him.

"Okay, Julián. We'll have to set up the date. How about in two weeks? Is that good enough?" he asked.

"What if the cancer cells move out of the prostate between now and then? Can we do it earlier?" I asked.

"That is impossible, Julián! I have to get everything and everybody in my staff ready. I'm sure we'll be ready in two weeks. The cells are not too aggressive. You'll be okay," he assured me.

"Okay! I'll be ready, too!" I told him.

"Fine, we'll see you, let's say, Thursday in two weeks," he stated.

We said good-bye to Dr. Lewis and got on our way back home full of trepidation. I couldn't control the fear of the cancer cells moving out of the prostate and, seeing the worry on my face, Teresa and the girls tried to ease those fears.

"You'll be okay, honey," Tere said. "By the way, he spoke of the side effects of a radical prostatectomy. What are they?" she asked.

"I will tell you about them when we get home. It's a little embarrassing. I don't want the girls to hear them.

Once at home and Tere and I were alone, she was anxious to know about the side effects.

"Now can you tell me what you didn't want to tell me in front of the girls?" she asked.

"Yes, honey, I can tell you. I'll tell you about the worst ones. In older men whose prostate is cut out, their ability to be intimate with their spouses may be lost. Also, a catheter is inserted into the male genitalia with a bag into which the bladder will empty. The whole thing is hidden under a pants' leg. Most men carry that contraption for only three or four weeks but a few have to carry it all their lives. I hope I am in that majority."

"Oh, my God! Let's hope and pray that you are!" I can't see you carrying that bag forever!" Tere exclaimed.

During the following two weeks, there was a lot of anxiety in our household. There were several nights when I couldn't sleep. Though my fear never left me completely, I was able to make up my sleep during the day. The day finally came and we were off and running to Sharp Memorial Hospital in La Mesa, where I was immediately assigned a room. All the members of my family kept me company until I was taken to the operating room. I can't remember how long the surgery took but I woke up in another room with an I.V. tube attached to my arm and a catheter with a bag at the end of it attached to my right leg. When the anesthesia wore off, I was quite uncomfortable and that discomfort lasted for a week. By the end of that week, my stay in the hospital was more comfortable, as long as I stayed in bed. But then, I was forced to walk with all those attachments and that was really uncomfortable.

At the end of three weeks, I was discharged from the hospital but the tube and the bag remained attached to my leg for two more weeks. At the end of those two more weeks, we went back to the hospital where the doctor relieved me of the catheter. Wow! Was I glad to be rid of it!

Fortunately, the days, weeks and months went by without any worries about emptying my bladder, except for the fact that I have to empty it more often than before the surgery. Unfortunately, the other side effect did occur. I was 69 years old when my surgery took place and I guess that is considered too old to escape that side effect.

Neither Teresa nor I took that loss too well. We tried and we tried but it was not to be so. For a long time, she accused me of not loving her anymore. She also thought I had a mistress. It was hard for me to make her understand that what we had read in the book and what Dr. Lewis had told us was happening. I even tried Viagra and it was somewhat successful but I got such a terrible headache that I had to give it up. She finally got used to the idea and from then on, there has been nothing but more hugs, kisses and sweet words. It has been hard adjusting to that routine but, after about 4 years, we are okay with it. And I'm happy to say that, though our intimacy is not what it used to be before my prostatectomy, our deep love has not diminished. Our love and dedication to each other has remained intact. Once we got used to our new way of living, post my surgery, everything went on fairly well, except for our concern for Teresa's Parkinson's, which seemed to be progressing faster now.

For many years the shaking of her arms did not interfere very much with her daily living. But, gradually, it began to change her life as well as ours. Both her arms began to shake slightly more and more and she began to worry about her inability to perform daily activities. More medicines were prescribed. At one time, she was taking as many as twelve pills with no noticeable relief and it was taking a toll on our finances. Her private insurance had also rocketed where I was paying close to $1,000 per month. Fortunately, I was already on Medicare and my premium was less than $100.

At the beginning of 2005, her shaking was still bearable but by the end of the year, it was so bad she couldn't take it anymore. Both her arms and her legs shook violently, especially her arms. The shaking of her arms tired her so much that she cried constantly. One day, she even told me, "Sweetheart, I can't take this shaking anymore! I want to die! What can you do?"

"I can't do anything, honey. I'm really sorry. I wish I could do something to alleviate your shaking but I can't. Let's make an appointment with your neurologist to find out what we can do," I told her.

"Yes, Julio. Let's do it right away. You know how long it takes to get an appointment. There must be a lot of people like me. Call him now!" she demanded.

"Okay, honey. I'll do it. Let's hope he can get us an appointment real soon," I told her.

I did call and we were lucky. When I explained Teresa's desperate situation to the neurologist, he told me to take her the following week.

The following week did not come as fast as we would have liked it to come but it did. We got to his office and we didn't have to wait too long to see him.

"Teresa," he greeted her. "I can see your shaking and I can imagine how uncomfortable and hurtful your arms must be. There is no medicine that will take away that shaking but there is a procedure called DBS (Deep Brain Stimulation) that will take it away. I think I told you about it some time back. It's kind of risky because doctors will be working inside your head and possible side effects may occur. But Dr. Ott has performed that procedure on several patients in your situation and none of them have had bad side effects. Discuss it with your whole family and call me as soon as you decide for or against it," he seriously told her.

Tere had not qualified for Medicare on her own work merits but as my wife she did. Before we left the doctor's office, I asked him, "Will Medicare pay for this operation, doctor? I'm asking you because if it doesn't, making an appointment for this procedure will be useless," I added.

"Yes, it will," he answered. "Don't worry about the cost, Mr. Lorenzana. Medicare will take care of it," he added.

"Thank you, doctor. She'll be ready for the operation," I promised.

The following day, we got our daughters together and we told them about the DBS procedure and asked for their opinion.

"Dr. Silver told us that the only thing that will take away Mom's violent shaking is a procedure called DBS. He said doctors will get inside her brain if she decides to undergo the procedure. That is why we called you together to find out what you think. She has already told me that she wants to have the procedure done, no matter what. She says she would rather die than continue struggling with her shaking," I explained.

"Is that right, Mom? You're not afraid to take it?" Lilián asked her.

"I'm afraid all right, but I cannot live crying all day long because of how tired the shaking makes me," Tere answered.

"I'm against it, if my opinion counts for anything. I don't want you to die so early in my life! I love you and I want you with me for a long time."

"I'm sorry, sweetheart, but none of you know how the shaking bothers me. I know it's a dangerous procedure but I want to take it, hoping it will take away my shaking for at least five years," she said.

"What if you die in the operation, mom? The doctor said it was a very risky procedure," Leslie said.

"Yes, he did. But he also said that several patients in my situation have taken it and the procedure took away their shaking. He said those patients looked normal after the procedure. We've seen the video showing the results," Mother argued.

"Well, mom, if you are willing to take it, we should back you up and pray to God it is successful," Lilián stated.

"Okay, mom, I agree with Lilián," Susan piped in.

"Well, I still wish you wouldn't take it but, if that is what you want, I'll have to give you my permission," Leslie finally said.

"Your permission!" Susan and Lilián shouted simultaneously.

"She doesn't need your permission!" Lilián said. "But we're glad you're with us," she added.

"Okay, so we're all in agreement that she should take the procedure. Let's pray to God it will help her," Susan said.

"I'll call his office and ask when the doctor can perform the procedure," I told them.

The next day, I called the neurologist and asked him to set a date for the procedure as soon as possible. He gave me eight days because he said they had to get all the necessary things for the operation ready.

"June eighteen is the day of the procedure. Today is June 10 and school lets out on the June 12. That gives us eight days to get ready. That's a long time and I know you're going to get tired of that shaking but I couldn't get an earlier date. I just hope you can bear it, honey," I told her.

The following week was hell for Teresa and, to a certain extent, for me because I had to try to keep her comfortable and try to take her mind away from her torture. The night before the date, she had a hard time sleeping and so did I. I tried to lift up her spirits because she told me, "I'm tired of this shaking, Julián. Do something, please! Give me something to stop shaking! I can't stand it anymore! I want to die!"

"Please don't say that, honey! You don't want to die. If you die, what will we do without you?" I asked her.

"You all will be fine. You don't need me. Look. When I'm shaking, I can't do anything!" she complained.

"But you don't shake all the time and, at those times, you do a lot of things. Try to relax. Tomorrow is the day and after that, your shaking will be a thing of the past," I tried to console her.

"Thank you, Julián. I'll try to calm down and think about June 18," she promised.

The eighteenth came and we hurried to San Diego. We knew how anxious Teresa was to have the procedure done and how much she wanted to get rid of her shaking.

The doctors prepared her for the operation, which was to take place at 7 PM. She was taken to the operating room, leaving us with all kinds of bad and good thoughts. The operation was to take a long time so we waited in the waiting room until it was over. When they took her to the recovery room, we were allowed to see her but they suggested we go to the hotel because she was heavily sedated and would not be able to talk to us. She did open her eyes for a moment and, when she saw us, she gave us a faint smile.

"Hello, sleepy head. How are you feeling?" I asked her. But, of course, she couldn't talk so, again, she just gave us a big smile.

"We're going to the hotel to sleep but we'll see you early in the morning, tomorrow," Lilián promised. Teresa seemed to nod her head and smiled again.

When we returned to the hospital the next morning, she was quite awake. As soon as she saw us, she asked, "Where have you been?"

Leslie answered, "Mommy, we were here last night but we had to go to the hotel to sleep. Don't you remember?" she asked.

"No, I don't," she answered. "I must have been completely out," she added.

"You were not completely out because you gave us a big smile when we told you the doctors had told us we had to go to the hotel and come back today. They said you would not be able to talk to us," Susan told her.

"You didn't want us to stay in the hospital all night, did you?" Lilián asked.

"Oh, no, I'm sorry!" she answered apologetically. "I'm so happy to see you all!" she added.

"It's okay, sweetheart. We are here with you now," I told her.

"We are so happy to see you without your shaking!" Susan exclaimed. "Isn't it great? Aren't you happy?" she asked.

"Of course, I'm happy, sweetheart. I'm ecstatic!" she answered. "Let's hope it doesn't come back," she added.

"Are you in any pain, mommy?" Lilián asked.

"No, thank God! I feel fine." Tere answered.

We asked the doctor if we could take her home and he said, "Yes, she's ready to go home. I'm sure she will rest from her shaking for a long time. It may be gone forever," he added.

"We hope so," I told him. "Good-bye doctor and thank you for everything," I added.

We went to the hotel to pick up our things and we soon were on our way home.

Chapter 12

Dyskinesia Sets In

For a few years after her DBS procedure, the only things we were worrying about were her lack of balance, which was not affecting her daily living yet.

At first, her balance was not bad but we soon began to worry about it because she began to fall whenever she was standing still. At first, those falls were inconsequential but that soon changed. Soon, every time she was standing, I would warn her to be careful or would rush to her side to hold on to her and guide her to a spot where she would anchor herself or sit down. She continued to perform her daily chores without too much trouble for a few years.

For some time, her falls occurred from a standing position, for some reason. But one day, she tried to take a step and she couldn't make it. It was then that we noticed her muscles were beginning to really fail her. Again our daily routine was changed because, a few months later, she had to be moved in a wheel chair, especially whenever we went shopping. At home, we would simply have her do some leg exercises in order to tone her muscles and she was, usually, able to walk a little. She also began to use a helmet to protect her from heavy falls.

Though Teresa wore her helmet every time she was walking, we were extremely careful with her. There were many safety rules she had to follow and constant warnings were added to our daily routine. As long as she adhered to those rules, she was able to walk a little without too much trouble.

"Please wear your helmet whenever you plan to get up and walk, Tere. Don't forget!" I often told her.

"Okay, honey, I won't forget," she promised.

But once in a while, when I heard a loud thud on the floor I knew that she had fallen. When I saw her on the floor, my first reaction was anger.

"What happened to you? Did you fall?" I asked her. "Didn't I tell you to walk carefully?" I yelled.

"I was careful and I'm wearing my helmet. I don't know why I fell," she said. "I'm sorry, honey," she apologized.

"I'm sorry for yelling at you, sweetheart. I know it is not your fault," I apologized, too.

Chapter 13

Teresa in a Wheel Chair

Several episodes like this one were repeated for a few years until she could hardly walk by herself. Then, things changed drastically. Now she was forced to be on a wheel chair most of the time at home and, especially when we went somewhere out of the house.

"What are you trying to do, honey?" I asked her as I saw her trying to get out of her wheel chair one day. "Are you trying to get up?"

"Yes, sweetheart, I am but I can't do it," she answered. "It looks as if this blasted disease is trying to keep me from walking. Please help me get up," she begged.

"Okay, honey, I'm coming. Come on, give me your hands," I said. "There, you're up. Can you still walk by yourself?" I asked her.

"Let me try. I think I can. Yes, I can still walk. But I forgot my helmet. Get it for me, will you please?" she asked.

As soon as I put it on her, I grabbed her arm and she began to walk. She could walk, alright, a little wobbly but she could still walk, with some help. She experienced several falls a year, mostly with minor consequences, thanks to her helmet. And those falls occurred when she stubbornly tried to walk by herself.

One time, I was in our bedroom while she was in the living room when, suddenly, I heard her yell, "Sweetheart, come and help me up! I want to go to the bathroom!"

"I'll be right there, honey! Hold it a second!" I yelled back.

The next thing I heard was a soft thud on the floor. I rushed to her and found her on the carpet floor.

"What happened, sweetheart? You're on the floor so I assume you fell, right?" I asked her. "I'm sorry I couldn't come sooner," I apologized.

"Don't worry, honey. I'm okay. I tried to get up by myself but I think I lost my balance. It's a good thing the living room is carpeted. I scraped my elbow a little but nothing major," she said. "I will wait for you the next time I want to get off my chair," she promised.

Another time, while in her wheel chair, she bent over to pick up something off the floor and she tumbled forward, hitting her forehead. She opened up a gash that bled a little. I simply cleaned it, put on some Neosporin and covered the gash with a bandage.

The fall that really had bad consequences was when she tried to get off her wheel chair to shoo away some little boy who, supposedly, was in the living room trying to steal something.

"Sweetheart, come quickly. A little boy is stealing something. Hurry! Hurry!" she insisted.

"I'm coming, honey! But nobody is stealing anything! Don't try to get up!" I shouted.

It was too late. Teresa had gotten up, somehow. She tried to take a step but she couldn't and she fell.

"Tere, I told you nobody was here. You shouldn't have tried to walk. Now you know what the result was," I told her.

She was on the floor facing down. When I turned her around, I saw her mouth bleeding. To make things worse, she had three of her front teeth broken in half.

"Your mouth is bleeding and you have three broken teeth. I may have to take you to the hospital, honey," I told her.

"I'm okay, sweetheart. I don't feel bad. The only thing I feel bad about is my broken teeth and what it's going to cost you to replace them," she said.

"Don't worry about that, honey! We'll worry about that later. Right now, tell me how you really feel," I asked.

"I feel fine. My teeth or my gums hurt a little but I feel okay. I don't think I need to go to the hospital," she claimed. "What I need is my new teeth," she joked.

"You'll get them as soon as possible. Right now, I'll take you to bed so you can rest. I'll give you something cold to put over your mouth to keep it from swelling," I said.

Two days later, Teresa saw the orthodontist, who checked her and ordered a bridge of the three teeth to replace her lost ones. In about a month, she began wearing her new teeth, but not before a stern warning.

"Don't forget to be careful. Remember, there is nobody in the house except for you, me and our cat. So, even if you think you see someone in the house, don't try to get off your wheel chair, okay?" I told her.

"Okay, I'll try to remember. But if I call you, please come to me right away," she pleaded.

"You got it, honey!" I promised.

Chapter 14

Dementia Sets In

For quite some time now, Teresa has been able to avoid falling because she doesn't try to walk by herself but she has begun to imagine all kinds of things. She is constantly hallucinating. The second hint we got of her impending dementia was when she began to hide things. We had just returned from a shopping spree when I noticed she was hiding something.

"Tere, what are you doing with your change?" I asked her.

"I'm hiding it so that those children will not steal it," she answered.

"What children?" I asked her. "There is no one in the house, except for you me and our cat. Remember that you are sick and your disease makes you see things that are not there. Nobody, except for your daughters and your grandchildren, ever comes to our house," I told her.

"Oh, I'm sorry. I forgot about my disease. But I keep seeing things," she complained.

"I know. Just don't forget to get those thoughts and visions out of your head. I know it's hard. But try it, okay, so you won't worry too much," I said.

"Okay, I'll try." she agreed.

There have been other instances when her dementia took control of her mind.

One day we went shopping and, because the cashier had talked to me nicely, her normal jealous characteristic became quite abnormal as she asked me, "Why was that lady so nice to you? Is she your new mistress?"

"What on earth are you talking about? Why are you asking me that?" I asked her. "I don't have a mistress! I don't need one. I think you're hallucinating," I said.

"No, I'm not! I saw how you two smiled at each other!" she protested. "How many mistresses do you have?" she asked.

"I told you I don't have a mistress!" I protested. "Don't you give me everything I ask of you?" I asked.

"Yes, I do. But what does that have to do with anything?" she innocently asked.

"It has everything to do with what you are accusing me of. What is a mistress for? It has to do with sex, right?" I asked. "If you agree and you know that you never say no to me, then you will understand that I don't need the services of another woman. I've told you a million times that I love you and that I will be with you until death do us part," I reminded her.

"Oh, I'm sorry, honey. Please forgive me. I know you love me but this dementia of mine is always crossing me," she said.

There have been many instances when we would be talking and she would suddenly ask, "Where is Julio?"

"Why are you asking for Julio? I'm Julio, your husband. Who do you think I am?" I asked.

"You are Joe, Julio's brother. You're not my husband," she insisted. "Call him, please!" she pleaded.

"I'm your husband! Look at me closely!" I begged.

"Oh, yes. You are Julio. How silly of me. I'm sorry," she apologized.

I remember an incident that occurred sometime back when Teresa was just beginning to hallucinate. We happened to be eating breakfast when I told her, "We're going to the post office to mail my monthly payments. Then we'll go get some money at the bank. Next we will go pick up your medicines at Vons. Finally, we'll go to Walmart to pick up some groceries."

"Okay. Can we go get some hamburgers after that?" she asked.

"Sure," I answered. "But we'll have to bring them home so we won't have to buy the drinks," I added.

"That's okay," she agreed. "I don't mind that. I feel more comfortable eating at home," she added.

On the way to Walmart, after having gone to the post office, the bank and Vons, she started crying and saying at the same time, "You're mean!"

"Why am I mean? What are you talking about?" I asked.

"You are wasting time on purpose! We need to go home! They are destroying our house!" she exclaimed.

"Who is destroying our house? And how do you know?" I inquired.

"The boys are!" she answered.

"What boys? There's nobody destroying our house! You're imagining it. The house will be okay. Don't worry," I tried to calm her down.

When we got to Walmart, Tere, again, said, "Can we go buy some hamburgers?"

"Sure, why not? I'm hungry, too," I answered.

On our way back from Walmart, we passed by KFC and she said, "Let's buy some Kentucky fried chicken, instead!"

"What about your hamburgers?" I asked.

"Forget about them! We haven't eaten fried chicken in a long time," she answered.

"But I thought you told me recently that we have been spending too much money lately. If we buy fried chicken, it's going to cost more than the hamburgers," I told her.

"It doesn't matter! I feel like eating fried chicken!" she shouted.

"Okay. Fried chicken it will be," I said.

When we got home, she saw the house and said, "Oh, the house is okay! I was wrong. I guess my mind does play tricks on me as you have told me. I'm sorry."

"It's okay, honey. Forget about it," I told her.

She had forgotten the idea that our house was being destroyed but her mind was constantly playing tricks on her. Those tricks went from bad to worse and when she began hiding things, we often had discussions about those tricks in attempts to get them out of her mind.

"Tere, try to remember not to hide things because later, we can't find them. There is never anybody in our house. We're always alone, except for our cat. Remember when you hid our car keys and we had a hard time finding them?" I asked her.

"Yes, I remember," she agreed. "I also remember that we needed to go to the store and we couldn't find them. Finally, we found them when I was looking for my shoes," she added.

"Yes, we did. I don't know what we would have done if we hadn't found them. Now you do understand how important it is not to hide things, right?" I asked her.

But, of course, she would not remember because she went on hiding things and, eventually, her hallucinations included other things. Now she doesn't hide anything because she doesn't think she has anything worth stealing. Actually, she just doesn't think, as she has lost her cognitive skills. Now she has other problems, of which she is not aware.

Her disease progressed slowly at first but now, after thirty-three year of suffering with the disease, things have gotten worse.

The hiding episodes are in the past. The accusations of me having mistresses have disappeared, too, and for her, that kind of anxiety is gone. Now, mostly frustration bothers her quite often. As for me, my sleepless nights are not too bad anymore and the anger and indignation I felt when I was accused of having mistresses and sex on the living room carpet floor are gone.

Recently, the workload of caregiving has become too much for me because she has lost her cognitive skills. She cannot reason anymore and she has lost control of her bowel movements. That has created more work for me. Now, I have to dress and undress her. I have to clean her pee and her poop. And these chores wouldn't be so bad if she did numbers one and two normally and in the regular toilet.

I was having lots of trouble helping Teresa in and out of the shower, probably because she was losing her cognitive skills, so, to make my job easier, I installed three bars in the shower room, placed in convenient spots. I placed two inside the shower and one by the toilet. I firmly believed she was losing her cognitive skills the next time I helped her take a shower. On that day, we were on the way to Jack-in-the-Box when she told me, "I need to go to the bathroom!"

"Well, we'll have to go back home. Even though there is a bathroom at Jack-in-the-Box, going to the bathroom in the house is more relaxing," I said.

"Yes, it's true," she agreed.

When we got home, I wheeled her to the bathroom. I got her to the toilet and, as I began to help her take off her underwear to sit her on the toilet seat, I noticed poop on her panties, on her pants and all over her derriere. This is the time when I became certain that she was losing control of her bowel movements, too. I used to simply clean her bottom using wipes but this was the first time I had to get her into the shower to clean her.

"Sweetheart, don't sit down. If you do, the toilet top will be full of poop. I will clean you as well as I can. Oh, heck! You will have to take a shower because I don't think I was able to clean you completely. Is it okay?" I asked her.

"Sure. I don't mind taking a shower. Help me into the shower," she asked.

"Okay. You're facing the toilet so I'll help you turn around. There. Now take two steps forward. Now stretch out your right arm and grab onto the bar on the right of the shower head. Do you see it?" I asked.

"Yes, I do. And I can reach it," she answered.

"Okay. Get closer and hold on to it with both hands. Now, jump over the little entrance wall with your left foot followed by your right foot and, as you do, grab the bar on the wall on your right with your right hand. That's it. You're doing fine. Now, grab the bar with your left hand, too, and hold on with both hands. Now, scoot over to the far end of the bar. Give me your left hand and step back a little. Now let go of your right hand and sit down on your shower seat right behind you," I said.

"I won't fall, will I?" she asked.

"No, you won't because I'll be holding you by your left hand all the time," I assured her. "That's right! You did it! Now, I will turn on the shower and you wash yourself as well as you can. I will help you finish the job as soon as you do your part," I told her.

I turned the shower on and she began to wash herself. When I realized that she had not done a good job, I finished showering her. When I finished washing and rinsing her, I turned off the shower and told her, "Now, here is your towel. Dry yourself as well as you can and call me when you finish."

A few minutes later, she called, "I finished!"

"Okay. Now, I'll help you get up. Here we go. As I help you up, get a hold of that bar on your right with your right hand. It's right there, left of the shower head," I told her. "Do you see it?" I asked her.

"Yes, I do. I got it!" she exclaimed.

"That's great! Now, grab the bar with your other hand. That's it. Now, face the bar and hold on with both hands so that I can dry your back. You dried as much as you could while you were sitting on the shower chair. Now, I will finish drying you before I get you out of the shower. Now, let go of your left hand so you can turn a little toward me. That's it! Now, grab the bar on the right of the shower head and do the same with your other hand and hold on. Good! You've done it! Now, give me your left hand first and then your right one and turn toward me. Now take a step forward and jump over the entrance to the shower, first with your left foot and then with your right one, and grab onto the bar on the left side of the toilet.

"I can't jump over it!" she complained.

"Sweetheart, you've been doing it since I started helping you into the shower. Come on, try it! I'll be holding you. Get your right foot out of the shower first and then your left one. Now grab the bar with both hands. Good! Now, I will dry the rest of your body so you can sit down. Okay, let go of the bar and I'll help you sit down on the toilet top. Finally, I'll help you put on your clothes and we'll be out of the bathroom. There, we're finished! I told you we could do it. We've been doing it for some time now but sometimes you get a little too stubborn or too scared to help me get you in and out of the shower," I reminded her.

"I'm sorry, honey. I just don't remember how to do it by myself. I'll try to remember all those steps we took to get me out of the shower. I promise," she assured me.

But she did not remember the next time I helped her take a shower. In fact, sometimes she got even worse. But thanks to God, I now have someone to help me almost all day long doing a lot of the things I had to do before.

This was also the time Teresa began to drool. That drooling got rather excessive so we went to see her neurologist. When he saw her drooling, he asked her, "Teresa, you are drooling more than you did the last time I saw you. Wouldn't you like to get rid of it?"

"Of course, doctor, but how can that be done?" she asked.

"I can give you some botox shots. They do a pretty good job of drying up your saliva so you won't have that problem," he answered.

"Will they really work?" I asked him because I had heard of botox shots taken for cosmetic reasons only.

"Yes, they work. She will have to take six injections, three behind one cheek and jaw and three behind the other cheek and jaw," he answered.

"Are they very expensive?" I asked him.

"Yes, they are. But don't worry about the cost. Medicare will be paying for them," he answered. "But will she agree to take them?" he asked.

Tere was listening so she answered, "Yes, I'll try them."

We visited the doctor every three months and the next three times we visited him, she was given the botox injections with really fear-producing, long, thin needles. After those three times, she didn't want to take any more because she was afraid of the needles and because the effect didn't last very long.

When she quit taking them, her doctor was rather unhappy. Probably, for that reason, he began to lose interest in treating her. We, likewise, lost interest in him because he seemed to be more interested in the money than in treating her. Another reason he might have lost interest in her was probably because there was nothing he could do for her anymore, besides monitoring the stimulators that control the electrodes implanted in her brain. So, we left him and chose another neurologist, a female this time. Unfortunately, she cannot do much for her, either.

Chapter 15

Dementia, Dyskinesia and Loss of Voice

As mentioned before, Teresa has been able to avoid falling, simply because she doesn't try to walk by herself but her dementia has gotten so bad she is still constantly fantasizing.

Recently, we went to bed at 8:30 and fell asleep at around nine o'clock. At one o'clock in the morning, Tere woke me up.

"What's the matter? Why are you awake? What do you want to do?" I inquired.

Her speech is quite bad at times. It is very soft and she mumbles so much, it is very difficult to understand what she wants to say. And if she tries to talk while crying, it is even more difficult. Maybe we'll understand one or two words but the gist of her message is lost. This time, I understood that she wanted to go pee so I got her up and put her on her little commode. After she did number one, I helped her off the commode, changed her special underwear and put her back in bed. As I tried to go to sleep, she, again, started moving around trying to grab the railings I put on her side of the bed for safety purposes.

"What do you want to do now?" I asked her.

"I want to get up," she seemed to say.

"Why?" I asked her. "It's only one thirty in the morning. It's time to be sleeping. Try to relax and go to sleep," I suggested.

"No! I want to go see Lilián!" she seemed to say.

"She's in Colorado. She's not here," I told her.

All of a sudden, she began to cry and, at the same time, she tried to say something. This time, it was impossible to understand her.

"Tere, if you want to tell me something, stop crying. I've told you that it is hard to understand your speech, especially when you're crying. If you want to say something, try to do it without crying," I explained to her.

When she stopped crying, she seemed to say something about the bathroom.

"Do you want to go to the bathroom?" I asked her.

"Yes," she answered.

"But you just went!" I told her. "Please relax and try to go to sleep. We should be asleep. I need to sleep. You know I can't make up my sleep late in the morning. You can sleep until nine or ten but I can't. Please try to go to sleep," I begged.

A little later, another period of wailing began. "Let's go see Leslie," she seemed to say at the same time she was sliding under the railing, trying to get out of bed by herself.

"Look, I'm going to get you up but only to give you your medicine. It's time for you to take it. Maybe it will help you relax and you'll go to sleep," I told her.

I took the railing off the bed, got her up, gave her the medicine and put her back in bed. She still seemed to want to get up but, putting my arm around her, I told her, "Relax, honey. You need to go to sleep." She didn't say anything but she soon relaxed and before I knew it, she was fast asleep. Then, it took me about fifteen minutes to fall asleep, as is usual for me.

Chapter 16

Living with Leslie

We don't go through these kinds of nights as often as we did when we were living in our house. Now that we live with Leslie, Teresa's babysitter comes earlier and leaves later. She now does most of the chores I had to do before and it's a great relief. For some reason, I also sleep better at night and I find myself with more time to myself. Unless I work on my writing or go to the stores, I simply sit down keeping an eye on her. I can't say we talk to each other because we can't. It has become impossible due to the fact that her speech is indecipherable most of the time.

It breaks my heart to see her so distanced from reality most of the time. I can't imagine how much worse our lives will become and I don't want to think about it. I will just wait and hope God gives us both the strength and the courage to bear whatever His will is.

There was a time a few weeks ago when she looked so much better. I thought maybe we were witnessing a miracle. She looked very alert, with her eyes wide open. We could understand her speech much better. She didn't look too sluggish and she was always smiling. But miracles happen to very poor, ignorant and humble people. Nowadays, miracles would never happen to sophisticated, well-educated and vain people. But, what does this well-educated, not very poor, quite vain person know about miracles?

We put the possible miracle aside because, the next day, she went back to her old self--the immobile, forward drooping, sideways leaning, tongue-out Teresa, who sits on her wheel chair most of the time, with a few sittings on the sofa. This has been her existence for about a year.

The times when she looks alert come and go, as was true a few minutes ago, when my daughter, Leslie, turned on some Andrew sisters' music and picked her up to dance. She looked very happy, probably because her daughter took time out to entertain her and because of the fond memories she has about the Andrew sisters, whose records we always enjoyed when we were young.

At other times, she is either lost in her world, actively fantasizing, crying or fiddling with parts of her wheel chair or with the floor. And, of course, we can't forget the situations she creates with her uncontrollable bladder or bowel movements. But what can we do? If she could help it, she would. But that dreadful disease is in control of her body and it will do so until a real miracle occurs or God decides to call her. We are here to help her make the ravages of her disease more bearable. It was a very pleasant sight, seeing Teresa "dance" with a big smile on her face. She never became a very good dancer but she loved to dance.

As stated above, she simply sits in her wheel chair, on the sofa or lies down on the sofa or on her bed. Once in a while, either the babysitter or I walk her around the living room. Also, either one of us spoon-feeds her when she's hungry or takes care of her bathroom needs but her babysitter helps her with her showers. We can do many things to help her offset her physical liabilities but for her cognitive skills, there's not much we can do.

This morning I noticed on the baby monitor that Tere was awake so I went to get her out of bed. I was giving her her morning medicine and, as she opened her mouth, I noticed that last night's medicine was plastered all over her tongue and lips. When I gave it to her last night,

I checked her mouth and didn't see any traces of the medicine so I assumed that she had swallowed it. I always remind her that if she fails to take her medicine as prescribed, it may have bad side effects. And sure enough, this morning she looked very lethargic and she even had her tongue sticking out. I don't know if those are side effects or not.

Later, while in the kitchen, her babysitter tried to give her water to wash off the medicine residue off her tongue and lips but Teresa grabbed the bottle and wouldn't let go. I took over and tried to take the bottle away from her but, in our struggle, it was squashed into nothing as it spilled the water all over the floor.

To find out if her blood pressure had caused her outburst, I checked her pressure but it wasn't very high. I still don't know what caused her rebellious outburst. I assumed it was simply her dementia causing her to fantasize about so many things.

Just last night, I woke up and found Tere kneeling on the floor just at the edge of the bed, almost naked. She was able to get down because I had forgotten to put the railing on her side of the bed. She had her clothes in her hands and there was a puddle of urine on the floor.

"What are you doing without clothes? There's a puddle of some liquid on the floor. How did it get there?" I asked her.

"I'm huh, huh, I want huh, to…I don't… know," she seemed to say.

"Why do you have your pajamas in your hands? Do you want me to help you put them back on? Where do you want to go?" I asked her.

"I…huh, huh, don't, huh, know." she seemed to say as she started to cry.

"Please don't cry, honey. Let me help you put on your pajamas and clean underwear. It's only four o'clock in the morning. You can't go anywhere except to sleep. Come on, let me help you up to bed," I said.

"No, let me be!" she complained and she began to cry again.

"Please, Tere, we can't go anywhere now. Let's go to bed. Let's wait until the sun comes up," I begged.

"Okay," she agreed.

I helped her to bed and she soon fell asleep. Once she was asleep, I cleaned the floor and tried to go back to sleep but I couldn't. By that time, it was already five o'clock so I got up to do whatever chores I had to do.

Because of her inability to speak clearly and in sentences and the lack of power in her speech, for the last few months we have not been able to understand what she wants to tell us. We can hear one or two words but the gist of the message is lost. We always try to guess what she is trying to tell us. Once in a while, her speech is clearer and more understandable. And when her speech is clearer, it's usually to say things like, "Let's go home!" "Where's Julio?" "Is your mother coming?"

Teresa has experienced some relief from her fantasizing, although she still fantasizes occasionally. They are now more on the quiet side. She doesn't show any excited emotion anymore when she fantasizes. As for me, I don't have those exhausting chores I used to have before we came to live with my daughter. Now most of those chores are performed by her babysitter, who is with us every day for seven or eight hours.

When we were living in our house, my job of caregiving was harder than it is now. I would wake up at four or five o'clock to do my stretch exercises, prepare our breakfast, work on the computer or watch TV for a while. At around nine o'clock, I would wake Teresa up, give her her medicine and wheel her to the kitchen. I would then prepare food and spoon feed her on her wheel chair or on the table. After her breakfast, I would sit her on the sofa and I would sit down with her for a while or I would do some of my chores.

When lunch time came, I would feed her and then we would sit down to watch some TV program. Of course, she would simply fiddle with parts of the sofa because her short attention span did not allow her to pay attention to the program.

At around four or five I would help her take a shower. As I mentioned before, this was the chore that required all my patience and strength. With my knee problems, it was a very tiring and painful ordeal for me.

At around six, I would prepare something light for us to eat. Two hours later, we would go to bed, where she would be relaxing while I watched some TV program for a while. As soon as she fell asleep, I would turn the TV off and go to sleep myself.

Chapter 17

Is It a Tumor or Not?

The problems caused by Teresa's disease are nothing compared to the problems that will come if this dark cloud hanging over my head drops its dark contents. If it does, it will create great problems for the whole tribe but especially for Leslie, Ben and Maya. To prepare for them, Leslie and I have been discussing the origin of that dark cloud and how to alleviate at least some of the problems it will create.

"Leslie, I've had a problem for the last two years that has me worried," I told her. "I finally went to see a doctor," I added.

"What is it? What's the matter?" she asked.

"When I'm eating, if I don't follow the last mouthful with some liquid, part of the food gets stuck in my throat and I have to cough it out," I told her.

"Why did you wait so long to see a doctor about it?" she asked.

"I was afraid I would get some tube down my throat. I've had that done before and I didn't like it," I explained.

"But you needed to have your throat checked from the beginning," she said.

"Yes, I know, but I told you why I hadn't done it," I said.

"And what happened? What did the doctor tell you?" she asked.

"He sent me to Pioneers Memorial Hospital to get some x-rays of my throat," I answered.

"And what happened? What did the x-rays show?" she asked.

"They showed a tumor," I answered. "Now I have an appointment at the hospital to get an endoscopy to perform a biopsy. The biopsy will tell the doctor if the tumor is benign or malignant. I am kind of scared because, whether it is benign or malignant, it will have to be taken out. It will, of course, be worse if it is cancerous because that will mean chemo and everything that goes with it."

"Try not to worry too much, dad. With God's help, it will turn out to be benign. Have faith in God," she suggested.

"I have it but if He thinks it's time for me, after eighty-three years, to go see Him, He will take me. That will be a big blow to your mom and to the whole tribe. And it will be a big inconvenience for you, Ben and Maya because you will have to put your mom in a nursing home, which will be a complete change for her. You will also have to take care of my things," I told her.

"Yes, it will be but let's not think of the worst now. Let's think that you will still be here to be around the love of your life and with the whole family who loves you," she said.

"Yes, of course. We'll find out about the tumor from Dr. Arabela on Tuesday, June 30, 2015," I said. "I'll try to be more positive but I'm scared," I admitted.

"I understand, dad. You will be okay. You still have a long time to live. Let's, instead, talk about what I will have to do if the unexpected happens. Since I would become the trustee, I want to be prepared," Leslie said.

"What are you worrying about? Everything is in our Living Trust. It states that you will make the decisions," I said.

"Yes, but since none of us, Lilián, Susan or I, will be able to take care of Mom, she will have to be placed in a nursing home and I will have to pay. Where will I get the money to pay for it. The money from the sale of your house is in your names. How will I get the monthly payment money?" she inquired.

"The Living Trust names you as the trustee but I suppose I'll see a lawyer to find out how you can prove you're the trustee. I'm going to see Mr. Patrick Pacey today for that purpose. We'll see what has to be done, so don't worry," I answered.

"Okay. I need to be prepared. You will be around for a long time so I shouldn't worry about it but I am. I'm sorry to worry you about it," she apologized.

"It's okay, Leslie. I understand your concern. Hopefully, we'll know what to do later today," I said.

As the day went by, my appointment with the lawyer at 3 PM was forgotten. I remembered about it at 7:00 p.m. and I had to confess my forgetfulness.

"Leslie, guess what happened. I had that appointment with the lawyer at three and I completely forgot about it," I told her.

"But how could you forget it? It was very important that you see him. What are you going to do now?" she inquired.

"I'll either call him or Dr. Suárez to see which one of them can help," I answered. "We can get a letter from Dr. Suárez confirming the fact that your mother cannot act for herself because of her advanced dementia. That should be enough," I added.

"Okay. I hope he can help," she said.

After our conversation, I called Dr. Suárez and his receptionist gave me an appointment for July 6, which is next Tuesday.

My appointment with Dr. Arabela went better than expected. He told me, "Julián, the endoscopy did not show anything. It seems as if you don't have a tumor. I don't know why the x-rays showed a tumor."

"Well, doctor, I'm really happy and relieved with your news. Now what will we do? Should we believe the endoscopy or what?" I asked him.

"Well, we'll have to repeat at least the x-ray to see what it shows this time. Next Tuesday is your appointment to get a second x-ray," he said.

"Okay, doctor. I'll take it even if I hate that liquid they forced me to take," I said.

So, here I am waiting for Tuesday of next week. God, help me!

"Well, today is Tuesday and I've had my x-rays done already. It's a chore taking those x-rays! That barium tastes awful! I almost vomited. But it's done. Now I'll have to worry for a while, waiting for Thursday to find out what the x-rays show," I told Leslie.

"Don't worry, dad. I don't think it could have been that bad. And it was necessary in order to better see what's wrong with your throat. I hope to God the X-rays don't show anything," she said.

"I hope so!" I told her.

Thursday came and when I went to see Dr. Arabela to find out about the results of my X-rays, he told me, "Mr. Lorenzana, your X-rays still show that you have something in your throat. I don't know what to make of it. The endoscopy did not show anything but the X-rays did. I think I'll send you to get an MRI to find out once and for all if you really have anything in your throat. Is that okay with you?" he asked.

"I don't like the idea of going for one test and then going for another one but if an MRI is the only option left, I will get it. Just get me the date." I agreed.

Dr. Arabela goes out and a few minutes later he comes back and tells me, "The MRI is set for the twentieth of this month."

"Okay, doctor, I'll be there. See you after the twentieth. Thank you," I promised and I left.

A day later, I told Leslie, "I saw Dr. Suárez yesterday."

"And what happened? Did he give you the letter we need?" she asked.

"Yes, he did," I answered. "I had asked him if he needed to see your mom but he said it wasn't necessary," I added.

"That's good. I just hope that's all I need. Now let's hope and pray that your problem doesn't become a major one," she said.

"I'll find out on the twentieth. That's the day I'll get an MRI. I hope it doesn't show a tumor in my throat, or anywhere," I told her. Actually, I won't know the results until a week after my MRI when I see Dr. Arabela about the results," I added.

"Yes, I know. But don't worry. Everything will be okay," she said.

When the twenty-seventh came, Leslie and I went to see Dr. Arabela for the results of my MRI. I was worried but not as much as I was when I went for the results of my first X-rays.

"Good morning, Julián," Dr. Arabela greeted us. "How are you two this morning?" he asked.

"Good morning, Dr. Arabela," I greeted him back. "We're fine, thank you," I answered. "How are you?" I asked him.

"I'm okay, thank you. Well, it looks as if you are okay. The MRI didn't show anything. Aren't you relieved?" he asked.

"You bet I am! Thank you for the good news!" I said.

"You're welcome. Now you can get ready for that class reunion you were talking about," he said. "I will give you an appointment for you to come see me in three months. But, if you feel sick or you feel any changes in your throat, call the office and I will see you as soon as possible," he added.

"I will!" I promised. "Well, good-bye and thank you again," I said.

"Good-bye and you're welcome," he said.

Leslie and I then walked out of the room and came back home. When we got home, I gave Tere the good news and she just looked at me and smiled. I don't know if she knew the significance of the news.

Chapter 18

Frustration and Hopelessness

"Now that we live in your house, I find myself with very little to do. Mona is here from ten to five so she takes care of Tere. If I don't have to go to the stores, to the show, to the bank or to the post office, I have more free time and I get bored. I could watch the Laker channel but too many shows are repeated. Soap operas I hardly watch anymore because I don't want to get hooked on them. Also, watching too much TV hurts my eyes. To the show I go only on weekends and to the store I go maybe every three days. I don't have anything special to write on my autobiography, either. I don't post poems on Facebook anymore. I also find myself cooking less now," I told Leslie.

"Well, go visit Susan and her kids. She's not working right now. Remember, she's on school vacation. You could also visit your brother. He doesn't work anymore," she suggested.

"I don't want to visit Susan. She's usually visiting her mother-in-law. As for my brother, he's usually babysitting at his house or at his daughter's," I answered.

"Well, dad, I can't help you not get bored," she said.

"I know, Leslie. I'm just venting my frustration. But I'll survive," I promised.

As I look at Tere sitting in her wheel chair with her face looking down at the floor or at parts of the same, at times her tongue sticking out, I'm overwhelmed by a combination of pity, compassion and love for her. She seems so different from the way she was years ago. And when we try to get into a conversation, frustration sets in, especially on her. She begins to tell me something and, after one or two words, she stops and starts to cry. When I tell her something, almost the same thing happens. She looks at me as if to say, "I understand what you're saying but I cannot find the words to reply." Again, she begins to cry.

When this happens, the only thing for me to do is give her a hug and a few kisses in attempts to dispel the awful feeling she must be experiencing. Only after a few more hugs and more words of comfort will her feelings of frustration seem to vanish.

The happiness she always showed in the old days are forever gone. She's now almost always quietly sitting in her wheel chair or lying down on the sofa or her bed, at times giving the impression that she wishes she was dead. That's the reason why, when I wake up in the morning, I lean toward her to feel her heat. When I feel her warmth, I realize that she is still with us and I feel relieved.

When I try to wake her up, it takes quite long for her to wake up. Recently, she also doesn't seem to want to take her medicine. At night, when I give it to her, she keeps the two pills in her mouth, along with the water, forever. When I think she has already swallowed them, I put her back in bed and she falls asleep right away. It's only when I wake up that I notice the medicine splattered all over her pillow. At times, I think she may be having trouble swallowing, which is something that Parkinson's disease patients experience. But it cannot be that because during the day she swallows her food very well.

I ask God to please have pity on her and show His boundless compassion to her! She has suffered enough. Just this morning, she spent twenty minutes crying. We had gone to bed at 9:30 and I had to go to the bathroom at 10:15, 11:20, 1:30 and 3:30 because I had drunk a soda and my fiber drink before going to bed. At 3:35, she was awake so I decided to give her some medicine while she was urinating. Afterwards, I helped her back to bed and tried to catch up on the sleep I had lost by going to the bathroom so many times. Well, it was impossible to do so because she wouldn't go to sleep. Instead, she started crying and, at the same time, trying to tell me something which I couldn't understand.

"Why are you crying, Tere?" I asked her.

She answered with a lot of mumbling but I did understand the word "desesperación", which is a combination of helplessness, frustration, despondency, despair and desperation. I could understand her frustration because she cannot do anything. She cannot move around by herself. She cannot speak clearly enough to be understood. And, worst of all, she has lost her cognitive skills.

"I'm sorry, sweetheart! I can understand what you have been feeling for the last few months but I can't do anything. Try to forget your problems and try to relax so that you can go to sleep. And, above all, ask God for help. Only He can help you feel better or take away your malady," I told her as I began to cry with her.

After a little while, Tere fell asleep and I decided to have a one way conversation with God. "Since Tere seems to have lost the ability to talk to you, I have decided to do the talking. Right now, my Lord, only you know what the future holds for us. Despite our many old-age maladies, we seem to be in fairly good shape. She continues with her disabilities but she may very well live for quite a long time. As for me, besides my allergy problems, my neuropathy, my knee problems and my spinal stenosis, I seem to be fairly healthy. Only an unforeseen fatal calamity like broken bones, heart attacks or some other major illness will kill one or both of us. If none of that happens, we will remain together, living from day to day and hoping and praying that when our time comes, you will take us together or as close together as possible. Either way, our love will remain as strong as ever here on earth and beyond. In the meantime, give us the strength, the patience and the health needed to be able to withstand whatever suffering you may deem necessary to send us in order to test our faith. Because we don't know how much longer you plan to allow us to live, I feel I need to ask you to please show your compassion to her. Take away her frustration and her suffering. Either take her with you or give her more strength to bear the suffering you have placed upon her. And, at the same time, give me the strength, the patience, the compassion and the wisdom to be able to help her in any way I can, as long as you have her in that state of mind and body," I pleaded.

This situation, full of frustration and exasperation on both of us, continued for a few more months, with her muscles becoming weaker and weaker. The little speech she had left, became softer and less decipherable. Her eyes remained closed longer than before. Her legs became so weak it was difficult for me to keep her standing while she was holding on to the bed when I wanted to help her to bed or on to her little commode. Her baby sitter and I had thought we would have to change her from pull-ups to regular diapers so we could simply wipe her bud while she was lying down in bed.

Chapter 19

A Very Sad Farewell

Suddenly, the unexpected happened. On Sunday evening, March 3, our wedding anniversary, was the last meal Tere would eat. On Monday morning the next day, she wouldn't eat her breakfast but we thought she probably wasn't hungry. When she failed to eat her lunch at noon, I began to worry so I made an appointment for her to see a doctor the next day. The doctor told us that she had a sore throat and that was the reason why she couldn't eat. She was given an antibiotic shot and we were told to return the next day for another shot. When I saw that she looked worse the next day, I took her to the hospital instead.

The hospital staff took a few tests, including a CT scan, and we were told that she had had a major stroke that rendered her unable to swallow. She remained in the hospital for three days taking in only liquids venously. Her eyes were now always closed and she looked calm but gaunt and lethargic. The only sounds we heard from her were moans when she was changed position in order to prevent sores from forming on her body.

On her third day in the hospital, we were told that we would probably lose her in one or two weeks. For that reason, Father Edward Horning came to the hospital to give her the last rites.

The doctor at the hospital gave us two options to choose from concerning Tere's care. One was to insert a tube through her nose or her mouth into her stomach and another one through a hole on the side of her stomach in order to provide the nutrients needed. The other option was simply to take her home and keep her as comfortable as possible but with no nutrients or liquids provided. Because the first option was too invasive and she was in a semi-coma state, we selected the second option and took her home. The paramedics took her home in an ambulance and placed her in a hospital bed Accent Hospice had already placed there.

We had lots of help from Accent Hospice personnel. A nurse visited Tere often to check her vital signs, to keep us up to date on her condition and to administer some medicines to her and to teach my daughters how to administer them. The only times Tere would utter any sounds or open her eyes was when her position was changed to avoid any sores from forming on her body. The sounds we heard were moans with which, we thought, she wanted to let us know that she was in pain or that she did not like to be moved. The rare times when her eyes were open, they were not focused on anything in particular. Her breathing was rather heavy and uneven for a while and my heart bled not only because of her abnormal breathing but, especially, because of her not having eaten for so long. She was so thin by now. Just about anything about her apparent suffering had me in tears, at times openly and at times silently.

She was constantly surrounded by her loved ones every day. Some would stay all day long until late at night. This was hard on our daughters and me because we had no privacy with her. Some of them cried along with us, which was very nice. It is so hard to see someone in that situation and not be able to do anything to ameliorate her suffering, especially a loved one like my Teresa.

On Friday morning, March 22, her breathing became very soft and very uneven. She would take three or four breaths and not breathe for thirty or thirty-five seconds. The hospice nurse happened to be here with us and she told us that the end was coming. Tere opened her eyes, stared at the ceiling, opened her mouth as if to say something and she took her last breath.

At the end, just as during the previous twelve days, she was surrounded by mostly all her loved ones so we all gave her our sad good-byes before they took her to the mortuary. I don't know who hurt the most but I think it was me because I will miss her the most.

We had to wait for two weeks for the wake and the funeral to take place. We had the viewing on Thursday, April 4. It was a fairly sad affair, with many close relatives shedding tears.

The Rosary was read by two lady friends, Socorro Ruelas and Jolby Ruiz. They alternated reading the Rosary's five mysteries, with Los Viejitos (José Magaña, Salvador Pérez, Manuel Ruelas and me) singing the chorus and one verse of "Y No Le Creyeron" in between each mystery.

After the Rosary, we sang four songs, "Más Allá del Sol", "Un Día A La Vez", "Te Vas, Ángel Mío" and "Pescador". Then, I sang three of my own compositions, "Se Fue Lo Que Más Amaba", "Sellado Estaba Por Dios Bendito", and "Te Quiero Por Muchas Cosas". I was sure I would choke while singing them because those songs are about Tere or dedicated to her, but only once did I stop to regain my composure.

The cremation was on Friday, April 5 and the funeral took place the next day.

We said good-bye to her with tears in our eyes but with a mariachi singing "Está Sellado", the special song she and I danced to at our wedding fifty-seven years before. I think she probably enjoyed it because it must have brought her happy memories. The mariachi sang several other songs, including a good-bye song titled "Las Golondrinas".

After the funeral, we had a get-together at Susan's house, where we had a luncheon and one more hour of mariachi music. At around 10:30, Ben, Leslie, Maya and I went home, thus ending a very sad but a little cheerful affair.

Epilogue

Life is usually beautiful when one is young but it can become devastating when one becomes a victim of a life-threatening illness. When old age comes, it joins forces with that malady to render one unable to do things and the situation becomes overwhelming. That is exactly what has happened to Teresa and me. Sadness overwhelms me when I compare my existence with Teresa during our first twenty or thirty years of marriage with our existence today. I think of all the things we were able to do together then and nostalgia sets in. She cannot think anymore and, therefore, she probably can't remember anything. But perhaps she can remember some things and becomes nostalgic, too. I don't know but our present situation brings tears to my eyes. There were so many happy things we would do together when we were young. Our lovemaking was out of this world, for one. Also, we would dance every time we heard lively music. We sang with the church choir every Sunday. We would sing along with whoever was singing on the radio. Or I would get my guitar to play and sing popular songs or my own compositions. We enjoyed ourselves when we visited friends or family members or when they visited us. We went to parties or to official dance halls and danced away part of the day or night. We would go to the park to play games or to regular high school or professional basketball or baseball games. We would go to theaters to watch some movies or we would sit on the sofa at home and watch our favorite shows. Life was a blast then, even though we had some bad times, too.

The really sad times began about fifteen years ago when Teresa was forced into a wheelchair because her Parkinson's disease had taken away her mobility. The dancing stopped. A little later, her voice began to desert her but we still managed to do some singing.

A few years after Teresa began to lose her mobility, dementia set in as she began to lose her cognitive skills. She began to lose interest in many of the things she loved to do. Then she began to lose control of her bowel movements. From then on, our outings together ended.

I wasn't doing much better. When Teresa began to lose her mobility, enough to be placed in a wheelchair, our lovemaking vanished due to the prostatectomy surgery I had to undergo in order to eradicate my cancer. I was diagnosed with spinal stenosis and my neurologist wanted me to submit to surgery but a second opinion informed me that it wasn't necessary. Then, I was diagnosed with peripheral neuropathy. Also, because of my having to move Teresa around, my right knee began to bother me to a point where now I cannot walk without a walker. Because of having to use a walker and because she had many "accidents" on our way to the stores, she now has to stay home with her babysitter when I go to buy groceries. When I come back, my feet feel so bad I have to take my shoes and socks off to rest my feet for a while.

Because of the medical problems mentioned above, we can't dance, we can't sing in duets, we can't go to the show together, we cannot sing with the church choir, we cannot make love, we hardly ever visit anybody or we don't get visitors, nor can we go to our grandchildren's regular school games or programs.

Life got so bad that my caregiving job was getting harder and harder. And, though I didn't relish the idea of leaving my house, it was sold in order to be able to hire somebody to help me take care of Teresa. For almost three years we have been living with my daughter, Leslie, even though I didn't enjoy the idea of moving in with her because of the Mexican saying, "El muerto y el arrimado a los tres días hieden", which means (a dead person and a guest begin to smell in three days).

Well, so far, we have been getting along beautifully and life is a little better and easier but it is still monotonous. Teresa has no life at all. She spends most of her time sitting on the sofa or on her wheel chair. Her speech has practically disappeared so I cannot converse with her because I cannot understand what she says. I feel really bad when she tries to tell me something and I cannot reply to her because I don't know what to tell her. I feel so helpless seeing her so helpless herself that I have to hide the tears I feel like shedding. She also has to be spoon-fed and helped onto everywhere she needs to be. But that's nothing compared to what I feel when I am not able to exchange conversations with her.

My existence is more bearable now. Though it cost me almost all the money from the sale of our house paying two baby sitters to take care of Teresa, I had my knee replaced and I can now walk. Even though I have some eye problems, I can still drive to go to the stores or to the show. I can still sing but I haven't played my guitar in a long time because, even though my daughter's house is big enough, there is no place conducive to performing the music activities I was able to perform in my own house. The time I spend away from caregiving is spent at the computer, on the sofa keeping Teresa company, grocery shopping or catching a movie at the nearest theater once a week. In spite of these fun activities, I find myself selfishly wishing my Lord would call me. That wish was not granted but I am glad He did grant me my long-lasting one, that of allowing me to be her caregiver and avoid placing her in some nursing home where she would have felt abandoned, alone and unloved. Instead, on March 22, two months before her 78th birthday, He called her. A major stroke left her in a coma-like state, unable to swallow and she spent three days in the hospital and nine days at home without eating or drinking anything. Although we did not see any sign of suffering, I'm sure she did suffer as she heard all her closest relatives talking to her or crying as we tried to make her last few days as comfortable as possible. The thing that hurt me the most was seeing her going through twelve days without eating or drinking anything. I feel guilt-ridden because, of the two options the doctor gave us concerning her health, I took the one I thought was less invasive and more humane. May God forgive me if I was wrong.

About the Author

Julián Lorenzana was born in San Antonio Matute, Jalisco, México, in 1932. He came to the United States in 1945, supposedly to work in the fields as an agricultural worker but Uncle Sam did not allow it. Child labor laws in the U. S. did not allow children to work during school time until they were at least 16 years old.

So, instead, Julian had to go to school, eventually graduating from Brawley Union High School, from Imperial Valley Junior College and from San Diego State University with a Bachelor's Degree in Liberal Arts, an elementary school teaching credential and a Master's Degree in Bilingual Education. He taught school full-time for thirty-four years in fifth through eighth grades, retiring officially in 1994. He continued teaching as a sub for only six more years because he had to stay home to take care of his wife, whose Parkinson's disease had taken away her mobility.

While teaching, he took a course in Children's Literature that inspired him to write and publish six short stories: "A Boy Becomes a Man", its translation "Madurez Temprana de un Niño", "Puppy Love", "Pet Cat on a Hunt", "A Dream Comes True", "Until Death Do Us

Part" (which was republished as "Love You Forever"), and "Short Stories, Childhood Anecdotes and Easy Poems for Everyone".

He has also written more than 700 songs and many long and short poems. Eighteen of his songs have been recorded semiprofessionally with his voice. His long-time dream was to become a professional singer but his marriage derailed that dream. He shares some of his writings on Facebook and on WritersCafe.org.

www.ingramcontent.com/pod-product-compliance
Lightning Source LLC
LaVergne TN
LVHW041538060526
838200LV00037B/1038